Silhouettes of fate

Ayush Utsav

Dedicated to every artist, creator, and
innovator, who dares to dream, and
transforms those dreams into reality

Preface

In the delicate interplay of love, life, and fate, there exists a journey that transcends time, memories, and emotions. Silhouettes of Fate is a story that captures this intricate dance, weaving together the threads of love, ambition, loss, and the enduring spirit of the human heart.

The novel follows the life of Arhaan, a young man whose path is shaped by the complexities of first love, the challenges of personal growth, and the inevitable twists of destiny. From the innocence of adolescence to the trials of adulthood, Arhaan's journey is a reflection of the universal search for meaning and connection in a world that is often unpredictable.

Alankrita, the woman who becomes the focal point of Arhaan's emotional world, represents more than just a love interest; she embodies the enduring impact that certain individuals have on our lives, even when circumstances conspire to keep them apart. Their relationship, marked by moments of deep connection and painful separation, serves as a reminder that love is not always about happy endings, but about the lessons we learn along the way.

As the narrative unfolds, readers are invited to walk alongside Arhaan and Alankrita, experiencing their joys, sorrows, and everything in between. The story is not just about two people, but about the broader themes of life—how we cope with loss, how we find the strength to move forward, and how we reconcile the dreams of our youth with the realities of our adulthood.

Silhouettes of Fate is a testament to the

resilience of the human spirit. It explores how love, in its many forms, shapes us, and how the memories of those we cherish can remain with us long after they are gone. It is a story of acceptance, of understanding that sometimes the greatest love stories are the ones that live on in our hearts, even when the people we love are no longer with us.

As you turn the pages of this book, I hope you find within it a reflection of your own experiences, and that it reminds you of the beauty and pain that coexist in the tapestry of life. This is not just Arhaan's story—it is a story for anyone who has ever loved, lost, and found the courage to keep going.

Chapter 1

The Philosophy of First Love

Love, as a concept, is perhaps one of the most enigmatic and complex emotions that humans experience. It transcends time, culture, and language, becoming a universal truth that shapes our lives in profound ways. But what is love, really? Is it merely a chemical reaction in the brain, a result of evolutionary biology, or something far more profound—perhaps even spiritual? To understand love, one must first consider its various forms and the impact it has on the human experience.

Love manifests in many ways: the unconditional love of a parent for their child, the deep bond between friends, the passionate love between partners, and, of course, the bittersweet emotion of first love. Each of these forms carries its own unique set of emotions, challenges, and rewards. However, first love holds a special place in the tapestry of human emotions, often setting the stage for how we perceive and experience love for the rest of our lives.

First love is a rite of passage, a moment in time when everything seems heightened—colors are more vivid, emotions are more intense, and the world itself feels charged with possibility. It is an experience that is often idealized in literature, film, and art, capturing the innocence and purity of a love that is untouched by cynicism or the complexities of adult relationships. But with that purity comes vulnerability, as first love often leads to heartbreak, leaving an indelible mark on the heart.

The philosophical nature of love can be traced back to ancient thinkers like Plato, who viewed love as a powerful force that could lead one to a higher understanding of beauty and truth. In his dialogue "The Symposium," Plato presents the idea of love as a ladder, with physical attraction serving as the first step towards the ultimate goal of loving the divine or the eternal form of beauty. For Plato, love was a transformative experience, one that could elevate the soul and bring it closer to the divine.

Yet, love is not always so lofty. It is also a deeply personal and often painful experience, especially when it comes to first love. The first time one falls in love, the emotions can be overwhelming—there is the thrill of attraction, the joy of being with the beloved, and the agony of separation. These emotions are often magnified by the inexperience of youth, making first love a powerful and unforgettable experience.

First love is often characterized by a sense of idealism. The person we fall in love with for the first time seems perfect, their flaws invisible to our lovestruck eyes. We see them as the embodiment of all that is good and beautiful in the world, and we believe that this love will last forever. But as we grow older and gain more experience, we realize that love is far more complicated than we initially thought. We learn that people are flawed, relationships require effort, and not all love is meant to last.

The changes that occur in life as a result of love are profound. Love has the power to transform us, to make us better versions of ourselves, or to bring out our worst traits. It can inspire great acts of kindness and generosity, or it can lead to jealousy, possessiveness, and even cruelty. Love can be a source of immense joy, but it can also cause deep pain and suffering. This duality is what makes love such a powerful and fascinating emotion.

When it comes to first love, the changes it brings are often bittersweet. On one hand, first love can fill us with a sense of wonder and excitement, making us feel truly alive. On the other hand, it can also lead to heartache and loss, forcing us to confront the harsh realities of life. The end of a first love can be devastating, leaving us feeling empty and broken. But it is through this pain that we grow and learn, gaining a deeper understanding of ourselves and the world around us.

First love also teaches us about the impermanence of life. Nothing lasts forever, and this is especially true of first love. The person we fall in love with at a young age is often not the person we will spend the rest of our lives with. People change, circumstances change, and what once seemed like an unbreakable bond can eventually fade away. This realization can be difficult to accept, but it is an essential part of growing up.

The emotions associated with first love are intense and varied. There is the excitement of discovering someone new, the joy of spending time together, and the thrill of physical attraction. But there is also the anxiety of not knowing if the other person feels the same way, the fear of rejection, and the pain of unrequited love. These emotions can be overwhelming, especially for someone experiencing them for the first time.

The changes in life that result from first love are not just emotional but also psychological and even physical. First love can lead to a newfound sense of self-awareness, as we begin to see ourselves through the eyes of another person. It can also lead to changes in our priorities and values, as we start to consider the needs and desires of our beloved. In some cases, first love can even influence our future choices, shaping the course of our lives in ways we might not even realize.

But perhaps the most important lesson that first love

teaches us is that love is not just about finding someone to complete us. It is about learning to love ourselves and to accept the love that we deserve. First love can be a powerful mirror, reflecting our insecurities, fears, and vulnerabilities. It can force us to confront our own shortcomings and to grow as individuals. In this way, first love is not just about the other person—it is also about us and our journey towards self-discovery.

Philosophically, love challenges us to question the nature of reality and the meaning of existence. Love forces us to confront the mysteries of the human heart and to grapple with the complexities of human relationships. It is an emotion that defies logic and reason, yet it is also one of the most fundamental aspects of the human experience. Love connects us to others, but it also connects us to something greater than ourselves—a sense of purpose, a feeling of belonging, and a desire for transcendence.

In conclusion, love, and especially first love, is a multifaceted emotion that has the power to transform our lives in profound ways. It is both a source of joy and pain, a force that can elevate us to new heights or bring us to our knees. First love is a journey of self-discovery, a rite of passage that teaches us about the complexities of the human heart. It is an experience that leaves an indelible mark on our souls, shaping who we are and how we approach love in the future. And while first love may not always last, its impact is felt for a lifetime, reminding us of the beauty, the pain, and the profound mystery of love.

Chapter 2

A New Beginning: Arhaan's First Day at School

Arhaan sat on the edge of his bed, staring at the uniform laid out neatly beside him. The room was quiet, save for the soft hum of the ceiling fan, but his mind was anything but still. Today was the day he had been dreading ever since his father had announced their move. It was his first day at a new school—a place where he knew no one, a place that wasn't his first choice.

Arhaan's father, an IPS officer, had been transferred to this new city, uprooting the life Arhaan had grown comfortable with. It wasn't the first time they had moved due to his father's job, but this time felt different. This time, Arhaan was older, more aware of the complexities of starting over. He missed his old school, where he had friends, teachers who knew him, and a routine that had become second nature.

He sighed deeply, running a hand through his slightly curly black hair. It was one of those mornings where everything felt heavy—his thoughts, his emotions, even his own body. He glanced at the mirror on the opposite wall and saw a fair-skinned, chubby boy staring back at him, with dark, deep-set eyes that reflected the uncertainty he felt. His cheeks were round, giving him a cherubic appearance that he had always been a little self-conscious about. His hair, thick and unruly, seemed to have a mind of its own, and no matter how much he tried to tame it, a few curls always managed to escape, falling into his eyes.

He wasn't particularly tall for his age, but his decent height didn't stop him from feeling small and insignificant, especially on a day like this. The school he was about to attend wasn't the one he had hoped for. His grades, though not terrible, were just average, and that hadn't been enough to secure a spot in the prestigious institution he had set his sights on. Instead, he was headed to a school he knew nothing about, filled with students he had never met.

The thought of walking into a classroom full of strangers made his stomach churn. Arhaan wasn't good at making friends quickly. He was shy, reserved, and often felt like he didn't quite fit in with the other boys his age, who seemed to glide through life with an ease he envied. His friends from his old school had taken years to find, and the idea of starting from scratch was exhausting.

Arhaan's father had been up early, as usual. Mr. Sharma was a man of discipline, with a strict daily routine that rarely wavered. By the time Arhaan had groggily made his way to the dining table for breakfast, his father had already been dressed in his crisp uniform, his shoes polished to a shine, and his face set in the serious expression that rarely softened. Mr. Sharma was a tall man, with a commanding presence that made people stand a little straighter in his vicinity. His eyes, dark and piercing, missed nothing, and Arhaan had often felt like they could see straight through him, finding all the flaws he tried so hard to hide.

The relationship between Arhaan and his father was not an easy one. Mr. Sharma was a man who valued achievement, discipline, and strength—qualities he tried to instill in his son at every opportunity. But Arhaan wasn't like his father. Where Mr. Sharma was decisive, Arhaan was hesitant. Where his father was strong-willed, Arhaan was more of a dreamer, his thoughts often drifting to music, art, and the stories he made up in his head. This difference had created a distance between them, a gap that only seemed to widen as Arhaan grew older.

Breakfast that morning had been a quiet affair. Arhaan's mother had placed a plate of parathas in front of him, her eyes filled with the usual warmth and concern. She was the buffer between Arhaan and his father, the one who understood his sensitivity, his need for space. But even she had been more subdued that morning, her usual chatter replaced by a silence that spoke volumes. She knew how hard this move was for Arhaan, how much he dreaded starting over, but there wasn't much she could do to change it.

As they ate, Mr. Sharma had glanced at Arhaan's uniform, making sure everything was in place. "Make sure your tie is straight," he had said, his tone leaving no room for argument. "First impressions matter."

Arhaan had nodded, not trusting himself to speak. He knew his father meant well, that he wanted him to succeed, but sometimes the pressure felt overwhelming. The constant reminders to do better, to be better, weighed heavily on him, especially on days like today when he already felt like he was sinking.

After breakfast, Arhaan had retreated to his room, under the pretense of getting ready, but really, he just needed a moment to himself. He needed to gather his thoughts, to find some semblance of courage to face the day ahead. He sat on his bed, his uniform beside him, and stared out the window at the unfamiliar street below. The houses, the trees, the sounds of the city— all of it was new, and none of it felt like home.

He thought about his old school, about the friends he had left behind. They had been his safety net, the people who understood him, who accepted him for who he was. Now, he was on his own, and the thought of trying to find his place all over again was daunting.

Arhaan's father had knocked on his door a few minutes ago, reminding him that it was time to leave. The sternness in his voice had made Arhaan jump, and he had quickly pulled on his uniform, fumbling with the buttons in his haste. His hands had trembled slightly as he tied his tie, trying to get it just right, knowing that his father would notice if it wasn't.

When he finally stepped out of his room, his father had been waiting by the door, his eyes scanning Arhaan from head to toe. "You're ready," Mr. Sharma had said, and though his words were simple, Arhaan couldn't help but feel like they carried a weight of expectation.

The drive to school had been silent. Arhaan had sat in the back seat, his hands gripping his backpack, his mind racing with thoughts of what the day would bring. His father had driven with his usual precision, the car moving steadily through the morning traffic, but Arhaan hadn't paid much attention to the passing scenery. His thoughts were too loud, drowning out everything else.

As they neared the school, Mr. Sharma had finally

spoken. "Arhaan, remember what I told you. This is your chance to start fresh. Don't waste it."

"I know," Arhaan had replied, his voice barely above a whisper. He knew his father meant well, but those words had only added to the pressure he already felt. A fresh start—it sounded so simple, but Arhaan knew it was anything but. Starting fresh meant leaving behind everything he knew, everything he was comfortable with, and stepping into the unknown.

The car had pulled up in front of the school gates, and Arhaan had felt a lump form in his throat. The building was large, imposing, and filled with strangers. His father had turned to look at him, his expression unreadable. "I'll pick you up after school," he had said, and Arhaan had nodded, unable to find the words to respond.

Now, as he stood by the school gate, watching his father's car disappear into the distance, Arhaan felt a surge of emotions—fear, anxiety, and a deep sense of longing for the familiar. But beneath it all, there was a small flicker of hope, a tiny part of him that wondered if maybe, just maybe, this new beginning could lead to something good.

Taking a deep breath, Arhaan adjusted his backpack and stepped through the gates, his heart heavy but determined. This was his new life, and whether he liked it or not, he had to face it. As he walked towards the school building, he couldn't help but feel like he was stepping into a new chapter of his life—one that he wasn't sure he was ready for, but one that he knew he had to embrace, no matter how difficult it might be.

Chapter 3

The First Glimpse: Love at First Sight

The morning air was crisp and cool as Arhaan made his way to school, the weight of the day pressing heavily on his young shoulders. The walk from the car to the school entrance felt like a long, lonely journey. Each step echoed in his mind, amplifying the uncertainty that had settled in his chest. He had barely slept the night before, his mind racing with thoughts of what the day might bring. His heart was a confusing mix of fear and resignation, knowing that today would mark the beginning of something entirely new— whether he wanted it or not.

As Arhaan approached the towering school building, he felt his stomach twist into knots. The gates, tall and imposing, seemed to loom over him, casting long shadows that mirrored the doubts in his mind. Students, both new and returning, streamed through the entrance, their faces a blur of unfamiliarity. He felt out of place, like a small fish thrust into a vast ocean, struggling to find his bearings.

For a moment, Arhaan hesitated, standing at the edge of the entrance as if an invisible barrier held him back. The sounds of laughter and chatter filled the air, reminding him of the friends he had left behind, of the comfort and familiarity he had lost. His heart ached with the longing to turn around and run back to the life he knew, to the school where he wasn't just another new kid.

But there was no turning back. With a deep breath, Arhaan forced himself to step forward, crossing the threshold into this new world. He kept his head down as he walked, his eyes fixed on the polished floors, trying to block out the overwhelming noise around him. He felt small, insignificant, like a single grain of sand on an endless beach.

The corridors were lined with students, some clustered in groups, others moving swiftly to their classes. The walls were adorned with bright posters advertising various clubs and activities, but Arhaan barely glanced at them. He was too focused on finding his classroom, too consumed by the anxiety gnawing at his insides.

As he turned a corner, he nearly collided with a group of boys, their loud laughter making him flinch. They barely noticed him as they passed, their conversation carrying on as if he didn't exist. Arhaan swallowed hard, his throat dry, and quickened his pace, eager to find some semblance of refuge in his classroom.

The room, when he finally found it, was already half full. Students were scattered across the desks, some chatting animatedly, others scrolling through their phones. Arhaan slipped in quietly, choosing a seat near the back where he hoped he could blend into the background. He placed his bag on the floor beside him and took out his books, his hands trembling slightly. The unfamiliar faces around him made his skin prickle with unease.

The bell rang, signaling the start of the day, and the chatter gradually subsided. The teacher, a stern-looking woman with sharp features, entered the room and began the roll call. Arhaan's heart pounded in his chest as he waited for his name to be called, each second dragging on interminably. When it finally was, he responded in a voice that barely rose above a whisper, feeling the eyes of his classmates on him for the briefest of moments before they moved on.

The morning passed in a blur of introductions and instructions, but Arhaan's mind was elsewhere. He was acutely aware of every sound, every movement around him, but none of it seemed to register fully. It was as if he were watching everything from a distance, detached and disconnected. He tried to pay attention, to focus on what the teacher was saying, but his thoughts kept drifting back to his old school, to the friends he had left behind. It all felt so foreign, so different from the life he had known.

By the time lunch rolled around, Arhaan felt drained. He had kept his head down, avoided eye contact, and spoken only when necessary. He wasn't ready to try and make friends yet, wasn't ready to open himself up to the possibility of rejection. Instead, he spent lunch in the library, a quiet refuge where he could be alone with his thoughts. He found a corner far from the other students and sat down, staring blankly at the pages of a book he had pulled from the shelf.

The library, with its rows of books and soft lighting, was a welcome escape from the chaos outside. The quiet hum of the air conditioning and the faint rustle of pages being turned were the only sounds, and for a brief moment, Arhaan felt a small measure of peace. He didn't read, didn't even try to; the book was just a prop, something to keep his hands occupied while his mind wandered.

But even in the quiet of the library, his thoughts refused to settle. He kept replaying the morning in his head, dissecting every interaction, every moment of awkwardness. He wondered if the other students had noticed how out of place he felt, if they had seen through his attempts to appear calm and collected. The thought made his stomach churn with anxiety.

When the bell rang, signaling the end of lunch, Arhaan reluctantly put the book back on the shelf and made his way to his next class. The rest of the day passed in much the same way as the morning, with Arhaan doing his best to stay under the radar, to avoid drawing any attention to himself. By the time the final bell rang, he felt utterly exhausted, both physically and emotionally.

As he packed his bag, he noticed the other students gathering their things, talking and laughing as they made plans for the afternoon. He felt a pang of loneliness, a sharp reminder of how isolated he was in this new place. He slung his bag over his shoulder and walked out of the classroom, his footsteps echoing in the nearly empty corridor.

As he made his way towards the exit, something caught his eye. A flash of movement, a glimpse of someone standing by the window at the end of the hallway. Arhaan stopped in his tracks, his curiosity piqued despite his exhaustion. He squinted, trying to make out who it was, but the bright afternoon sun streaming through the window obscured his view.

He took a hesitant step forward, then another, his heart suddenly pounding for a reason he couldn't quite explain. As he drew closer, the figure by the window became clearer, and Arhaan's breath caught in his throat.

It was a girl, standing with her back to him, her long, black hair cascading down her back like a waterfall. She was dressed in the same uniform as everyone else, but there was something about her that made her stand out, something that drew Arhaan in. Her posture was relaxed, confident, as if she belonged here in a way that Arhaan could only envy.

He didn't know why he was drawn to her, didn't understand the sudden surge of emotion that welled up inside him as he watched her. She hadn't even turned around, hadn't seen him, and yet Arhaan felt as if the world had shifted slightly, as if something important was happening, though he couldn't quite put his finger on what it was.

He took another step forward, his heart hammering in his chest, and then she turned around.

Arhaan felt his breath hitch as their eyes met. Her face was as striking as her posture—fair as milk, with sharp, delicate features and large, expressive eyes that seemed to hold a thousand unspoken thoughts. Her gaze was direct, unwavering, and for a moment, Arhaan felt as if she could see straight through him, as if she could see all the fears, all the doubts that he had tried so hard to keep hidden.

She didn't say anything, didn't acknowledge him with more than a brief glance, but that single moment was enough. Arhaan felt something shift inside him, something he couldn't quite explain. It was as if the world around him had faded away, leaving only the two of them in that sunlit hallway.

Then, just as quickly as it had begun, the moment passed. She turned away, walking down the corridor with a grace that Arhaan could only admire from afar. He stood frozen in place, his mind racing to catch up with what had just happened. He had never felt anything like this before, never experienced such an intense, immediate reaction to someone he didn't even know.

As he watched her disappear around the corner, Arhaan realized with a start that his heart was still pounding, that his hands were trembling slightly. He didn't know who she was, didn't even know her name, but something told him that this girl, this stranger who had walked into his life so unexpectedly, was going to be important. Somehow, in some way, she was going to change everything.

For the rest of the day, and long into the night, Arhaan couldn't get her out of his mind. Her image stayed with him, haunting his thoughts, filling his dreams. He didn't know what it meant, didn't know if he would ever see her again, but one thing was certain—something had changed within him, something that couldn't be undone.

And as he lay in bed that night, staring up at the ceiling, Arhaan felt a strange mix of emotions—excitement, fear, curiosity—all tangled together in a knot that he knew would take a long time to unravel. But despite the confusion, despite the uncertainty, one thought kept repeating in his mind, over and over again.

He had to see her again.

Chapter 4

A Melodious Connection: The First Interaction

A few months had passed since Arhaan first set foot in his new school, and the initial anxiety that had weighed him down had begun to lift. The days slipped by in a routine blur of classes, assignments, and occasional interactions with classmates. Arhaan had settled into his new life, finding a quiet corner for himself where he could blend in without drawing too much attention. He wasn't popular, nor was he entirely invisible—he simply existed on the periphery, watching and learning.

But there was one constant in his thoughts that refused to fade: the girl he had seen on his first day, the girl who had stirred something deep within him. Alankrita. He had learned her name from a passing conversation between classmates, but he hadn't yet spoken to her. She was always there, though, lingering at the edge of his awareness, her presence as undeniable as the sun in the sky.

Alankrita was everything that Arhaan wasn't—

confident, poised, and effortlessly graceful. She carried herself with an air of quiet assurance that made people take notice. Her academic performance was stellar, her popularity evident in the way she moved through the school, always surrounded by friends. She was the class representative, a role that suited her perfectly. Every teacher seemed to have a soft spot for her, praising her intelligence and dedication.

Despite this, Arhaan couldn't muster the courage to speak to her. He admired her from afar, content to observe her in the moments they shared the same space. He would catch glimpses of her in the corridors, in the cafeteria, or during assemblies, but each time, he found himself unable to approach her. He was too aware of the gulf that separated them—he, the average student with nothing special to offer, and she, the shining star who seemed so far out of reach.

Yet, Arhaan had his own strengths, even if he didn't always recognize them. He had always been drawn to music, finding solace in the melodies that flowed from his fingers as they danced across the strings of his guitar. Music was his escape, a way to express the emotions that he struggled to articulate. His creativity was another outlet, a means of channeling his thoughts into something tangible. These were the things that gave him comfort, the things that made him feel alive.

It was during one of the school's cultural events that Arhaan's talents came to the forefront. A music competition was announced, and despite his reservations, Arhaan decided to participate. Music was something he loved, and though he wasn't sure how he would measure up against others, he knew that he couldn't let this opportunity slip by. It was a chance to do something that mattered to him, to step out of the shadows, even if only for a moment.

The days leading up to the competition were a whirlwind of practice and preparation. Arhaan spent hours perfecting his performance, pouring his heart into every note. It was nerve-wracking, but there was also a thrill in the challenge, a sense of purpose that made the anxiety worthwhile. He didn't tell anyone about his participation—he didn't want the added pressure of expectations. This was something he was doing for himself, something that belonged to him alone.

The day of the competition arrived, and the school's auditorium buzzed with excitement. The audience was a mix of students and teachers, all eager to see what their peers had to offer. Arhaan's heart raced as he waited backstage, clutching his guitar like a lifeline. He could hear the murmur of the crowd, the occasional bursts of applause as each performer finished their piece. His mind was a jumble of nerves and anticipation, but he forced himself to focus on the music, on the reason he was there.

When his turn finally came, Arhaan took a deep breath and stepped onto the stage. The bright lights blinded him for a moment, and he could feel the weight of a hundred eyes on him. But then, as he settled into position and began to play, everything else faded away. The music took over, filling the auditorium with its melody, and Arhaan lost himself in the rhythm and flow of the song.

For those few minutes, nothing else mattered. The audience, the competition, the pressure—they all melted into the background as the music became his entire world. He played with a passion that surprised even himself, his fingers moving with a confidence that he hadn't known he possessed. And when the final note faded into silence, there was a brief moment of stillness before the applause erupted, loud and enthusiastic.

Arhaan blinked, almost dazed, as he realized that it was over. He had done it. The applause washed over him, a wave of sound that made his heart swell with pride. He had taken a risk, stepped out of his comfort zone, and it had paid off. As he walked off the stage, he couldn't help the small smile that tugged at his lips. For the first time since he had arrived at this school, he felt like he had truly accomplished something.

The prize distribution ceremony was held later that afternoon, and Arhaan was awarded first place in the music competition. The trophy was a simple but elegant piece, a symbol of his achievement. As he accepted it, he couldn't help but glance towards the crowd, searching for a familiar face. His eyes found Alankrita, seated among her friends, and for a fleeting moment, their gazes met. He couldn't tell what she was thinking, but the fact that she was there, that she had seen him perform, sent a thrill through him.

After the ceremony, Arhaan returned to his classroom, his heart still pounding with excitement. The room was empty, the other students having dispersed to enjoy the rest of the day. He placed the trophy on his desk, staring at it for a moment, letting the reality of his victory sink in. It felt surreal, like a dream he might wake up from at any moment.

As he was about to put the trophy in his bag, he heard a soft voice behind him, startling him out of his thoughts. He turned quickly, his heart skipping a beat as he saw who it was.

Alankrita stood in the doorway, her dark eyes fixed on him. For a moment, Arhaan couldn't speak, couldn't move. It was the first time she had approached him, the first time they had ever been this close. She looked just as striking as ever, her long black hair falling in soft waves around her shoulders, her fair skin glowing in the afternoon light.

"Congratulations," she said, her voice clear and warm. There was a small smile on her lips, one that made Arhaan's heart flutter uncontrollably.

"Th-thank you," he stammered, feeling the heat rise to his cheeks. He couldn't believe this was happening—Alankrita, the girl who had occupied his thoughts for so long, was standing in front of him, talking to him.

She took a step closer, her eyes briefly flicking to the trophy on the desk before returning to his face. "You were amazing out there," she said. "I didn't know you played so well."

Arhaan struggled to find his voice, his mind racing to come up with something to say. "I—I love music," he managed to say. "It's… it's something I'm passionate about."

"I could tell," she replied, her smile widening slightly. "You really put your heart into it."

Her words sent a rush of warmth through Arhaan, and for a moment, he felt like he was floating. He wanted to say more, to keep the conversation going, but his nerves were getting the better of him. His mind was a jumble of thoughts and emotions, and all he could do was stand there, staring at her like a deer caught in headlights.

Alankrita didn't seem to mind his awkwardness. She glanced around the empty classroom, then back at him. "It's nice to finally talk to you," she said. "I've seen you around, but we've never really had a chance to speak."

Arhaan nodded, trying to calm the frantic beating of his heart. "Yeah, I've… I've seen you too," he said, cursing himself for how lame that sounded.

But Alankrita didn't seem to notice. She simply nodded, her expression thoughtful. "Well, I'm glad we did today," she said. "Maybe we can talk more sometime?"

Arhaan's heart skipped a beat at her words. Was she really suggesting that they talk more? That they become… friends? The thought was almost too much for him to process. "Yeah, I'd like that," he said, his voice barely above a whisper.

"Great," she said, giving him one last smile before turning to leave. "See you around, Arhaan."

And with that, she was gone, leaving Arhaan standing in the empty classroom, his mind reeling from what had just happened. He could hardly believe it—Alankrita had spoken to him, had congratulated him, and had even suggested that they talk more. It was more than he had ever dared to hope for, and the thought filled him with a mix of excitement and disbelief.

As he finally packed up his things and left the classroom, the trophy clutched tightly in his hand, Arhaan couldn't stop the smile that spread across his face. The day had been a whirlwind of emotions, from the nervousness of performing to the elation of winning, and now this—his first real interaction with Alankrita. It felt like the beginning of something new, something important, and for the first time in a long while, Arhaan felt a flicker of hope in his heart.

The days ahead were still uncertain, but one thing was clear—Alankrita was no longer just a distant figure in his mind. She was real, tangible, and perhaps, just perhaps, she was about to become a part of his life in a way that he had never imagined.

And as he walked home that evening, the trophy shining in the fading sunlight, Arhaan couldn't help but feel that this was only the beginning of something extraordinary.

Chapter 5

Blossoming Friendship: Arhaan and Alankrita

After the brief but meaningful exchange that marked their first interaction, Arhaan and Alankrita's connection began to grow in earnest. What started as a single conversation evolved into a friendship that would profoundly impact both of their lives. In the days that followed, the initial spark between them ignited into a steady flame, and their relationship blossomed into something much deeper.

Alankrita, with her beauty and intelligence, quickly became a central figure in Arhaan's life. She was not only the class representative but also a beacon of positivity and competence that drew the admiration of teachers and students alike. Her poise and grace were evident in everything she did—from her ability to manage class responsibilities with apparent ease to her effortlessly engaging manner during conversations. Her presence in the classroom was marked by a certain charm and authority, and her peers respected her not just for her academic prowess but for her genuine kindness and ability to connect with everyone around her.

Arhaan, on the other hand, was just an average student. His physical appearance was unremarkable, with chubby cheeks and slightly curly black hair that fell into his eyes. His academic performance was middling, and he often struggled to stand out in the sea of his more accomplished classmates. But despite these perceived shortcomings, his genuine nature and quiet determination set him apart in ways that were not immediately visible. His friendship with Alankrita would eventually become one of the most defining aspects of his school life, marking a significant shift from his previous experiences.

The transformation from acquaintances to close friends happened seamlessly. Alankrita's natural friendliness and Arhaan's shy but sincere demeanor made for a complementary pairing. Their conversations, once limited to brief exchanges, grew longer and more meaningful. They began to share their thoughts on various subjects, from their favorite books and movies to their dreams and aspirations. These discussions often took place during lunch breaks or after class, when they would sit together in a corner of the school yard, away from the hustle and bustle of their peers.

Their growing friendship was not without its challenges. Arhaan's initial self-doubt and insecurity sometimes made him question why someone as well-regarded as Alankrita would want to be friends with him. However, Alankrita's consistent kindness and genuine interest in him began to dispel these doubts. She was genuinely curious about Arhaan's interests and took the time to listen to him. Whether it was about his love for music or his passion for painting, she showed a deep interest in understanding what made him tick. This level of attention and care was something Arhaan had not experienced before and it gradually helped him gain confidence.

Alankrita, for her part, appreciated Arhaan's unique qualities. She found his quiet strength and thoughtful nature refreshing in a world that often seemed loud and demanding. His humility and honesty stood in stark contrast to the superficial interactions she sometimes encountered with other students. Their conversations were always engaging, filled with laughter and introspection. Arhaan's perspective on life, shaped by his experiences and personal challenges, provided Alankrita with a new way of looking at things. She valued his insights and found their discussions stimulating and enriching.

Their growing friendship was noticeable to others at school. Alankrita was often seen in the company of her usual group of friends, but she made an effort to include Arhaan in these social circles. She would invite him to join her and her friends during lunch or to participate in group activities. Initially, Arhaan felt like an outsider in these settings, but Alankrita's presence made him feel more at ease. Her friends, who were initially curious about Arhaan, soon came to appreciate his presence and the positive influence he seemed to have on Alankrita.

As their friendship deepened, Arhaan began to feel more integrated into the school community. His once-limited social interactions expanded, and he found himself more comfortable participating in class discussions and school events. Alankrita's encouragement played a significant role in this transformation. She would often push him to take part in activities he might have shied away from before, such as joining the school's music club or participating in a talent show. Her belief in his abilities motivated him to step out of his comfort zone and embrace new opportunities.

One particularly memorable event was the annual school talent show. Arhaan, who had always been passionate about music, decided to participate after much encouragement from Alankrita. He had been playing the guitar since he was young, and he had written a few songs of his own. Alankrita had been instrumental in helping him prepare for the performance. She had listened to his rehearsals, offered constructive feedback, and helped him choose the right songs to perform. Her support and enthusiasm were unwavering, and they made a significant difference in his preparation.

When the day of the talent show arrived, Arhaan was nervous but excited. Alankrita was there in the audience, cheering him on and offering words of encouragement before he took the stage. As he performed, he could see her smiling and clapping, and it gave him the confidence he needed to give his best performance. The applause and positive feedback from the audience were gratifying, but it was Alankrita's pride and excitement that meant the most to him. Her presence and support were a testament to the strength of their friendship and the bond they had built.

Outside of school, their friendship continued to flourish. Alankrita would often invite Arhaan over to her house for study sessions or just to hang out. They would spend hours talking about their favorite books, discussing their plans for the future, or simply enjoying each other's company. These moments were precious to Arhaan, and he cherished the time he spent with Alankrita. She had become a source of joy and inspiration in his life, and he was grateful for the friendship they shared.

As the months went by, Arhaan and Alankrita became inseparable. Their friendship was a source of comfort and strength for both of them. Alankrita's support helped Arhaan navigate the challenges of school and life, while Arhaan's presence provided Alankrita with a sense of stability and understanding. Their bond was built on a foundation of mutual respect, trust, and genuine affection.

Their friendship also had a positive impact on their respective families. Arhaan's father, who had always been somewhat distant, began to notice the changes in his son. He saw how Arhaan was becoming more engaged in school and how his confidence was growing. Although he didn't always express his feelings openly, it was clear that he was pleased with the progress Arhaan was making. Alankrita's parents, on the other hand, were happy to see their daughter surrounded by good friends and experiencing positive growth.

As the school year continued, Arhaan and Alankrita's friendship remained a constant source of joy and support. They faced the ups and downs of school life together, navigating academic pressures, social dynamics, and personal challenges. Their bond grew stronger with each passing day, and they continued to be a source of encouragement and inspiration for one another.

Looking back, Arhaan realized how much his life had changed since meeting Alankrita. She had become more than just a friend; she was a confidante, a source of inspiration, and a cherished part of his life. Their friendship had transformed him in ways he had never imagined, and he was grateful for the positive influence she had brought into his life.

As they approached the end of the school year, Arhaan and Alankrita continued to strengthen their bond. They had built a friendship that was both meaningful and lasting, and they were excited about the future and the possibilities it held. Their connection was a testament to the power of friendship and the impact it could have on one's life.

In the end, Arhaan knew that their friendship was one of the most important things in his life. It had helped him grow, find confidence, and experience joy in ways he had never thought possible. As they moved forward, he was confident that their bond would continue to be a source of strength and support, no matter where life took them.

Chapter 6

Strengthening Bonds: A Friendship Flourishes

As the school year progressed, Arhaan and Alankrita's friendship continued to deepen, evolving from casual acquaintances into close, inseparable companions. Their bond was solidified through shared experiences, mutual support, and a genuine affection that transformed their interactions into something truly meaningful.

Arhaan and Alankrita's friendship was characterized by its natural ease and comfort. They spent considerable time together, whether it was during lunch breaks, after school, or on weekends. Their days were filled with laughter, shared secrets, and meaningful conversations that drew them closer with each passing moment.

One of the most significant ways in which their friendship flourished was through academic support. Arhaan, who had always struggled with his studies, found himself benefiting greatly from Alankrita's help. She had a natural aptitude for academics and a deep understanding of various subjects, and she generously offered to help Arhaan improve his performance.

Their study sessions began with simple review meetings where Alankrita would assist Arhaan with his homework and explain complex concepts in a way that made them more comprehensible. These sessions often took place in the school library or at Alankrita's house, where they could work without distractions. Alankrita's patience and clarity made a noticeable difference in Arhaan's understanding of the material. She had a knack for breaking down difficult subjects into manageable parts, which helped Arhaan grasp the concepts more effectively.

Arhaan's grades began to improve gradually, and his newfound confidence in his academic abilities was palpable. He was no longer the student who struggled to keep up; instead, he became someone who could hold his own in class discussions and perform well in exams. This improvement was not just a result of Alankrita's tutoring but also her unwavering belief in his potential. Her encouragement and support played a crucial role in boosting Arhaan's self-esteem and motivating him to work harder.

Beyond academics, their friendship was enriched by their shared interests and activities. They both enjoyed music, and this common passion led them to explore new avenues together. Arhaan had always been interested in playing the guitar, and he often practiced during their time together. Alankrita, who had a keen ear for music, would listen to his practice sessions and offer feedback. Her appreciation for his talent was a source of encouragement for Arhaan, and their musical sessions became a cherished part of their friendship.

In addition to music, Alankrita and Arhaan discovered a mutual love for literature. They began to exchange books and discuss their favourite authors and genres. Their conversations about literature were intellectually stimulating, and they found joy in exploring new ideas and perspectives. These discussions often took place during their study sessions or casual hangouts, and they became a regular part of their interactions.

Their friendship also extended beyond the school

environment. Alankrita would invite Arhaan to various family gatherings and events, where he was warmly welcomed by her family. These occasions provided Arhaan with a glimpse into Alankrita's life outside of school and allowed him to form connections with her family. Her parents, who were aware of the positive influence she had on Arhaan, appreciated his presence and were supportive of their friendship.

Similarly, Arhaan began to include Alankrita in his family life. He invited her to his home for dinner and introduced her to his family. These visits were filled with laughter and lively conversations, and they helped strengthen the bond between their families. Arhaan's parents were pleased to see their son's growing confidence and academic improvement, and they valued Alankrita's role in his life.

Their friendship also saw its share of challenges and disagreements. While they were generally supportive of each other, there were times when their differing opinions led to conflicts. However, these disagreements were always resolved through open communication and mutual respect. They learned to appreciate each other's perspectives and find common ground, which further strengthened their bond.

One memorable instance of this occurred during a heated debate about a book they had both read. Arhaan had a strong opinion about the book's ending, while Alankrita had a different perspective. Their discussion became passionate, and they found themselves at odds. However, instead of letting the disagreement drive a wedge between them, they took the time to listen to each other's viewpoints and understand where the other was coming from. This open and honest dialogue allowed them to resolve the conflict and deepen their understanding of each other's thought processes.

Their growing bond was also reflected in the way they celebrated each other's successes. When Alankrita received an award for her academic achievements, Arhaan was genuinely thrilled for her. He attended the award ceremony with great enthusiasm and proudly cheered her on. Similarly, when Arhaan performed at the school's annual talent show and received accolades for his musical performance, Alankrita was there to offer her congratulations and praise.

These moments of mutual celebration were important milestones in their friendship. They not only showcased their support for each other but also highlighted the depth of their connection. Their ability to share in each other's joy and success was a testament to the strength of their bond.

As their friendship continued to evolve, they began to rely on each other for emotional support as well. There were times when Arhaan faced personal challenges or felt overwhelmed by the pressures of school, and Alankrita was always there to lend a listening ear and offer encouragement. Conversely, when Alankrita faced difficulties or felt stressed, Arhaan provided her with a sense of calm and reassurance. Their ability to be there for each other in times of need further solidified their friendship.

One particular instance stands out in this regard. Alankrita was going through a period of intense stress due to a major academic project. She felt overwhelmed by the workload and was struggling to balance her responsibilities. During this time, Arhaan made a conscious effort to be a source of support for her. He would often bring her coffee or snacks during their study sessions and offer words of encouragement. His presence and thoughtfulness were a source of comfort for Alankrita, and they helped her navigate the stressful period with greater ease.

As the school year drew to a close, Arhaan and Alankrita's friendship remained a central part of their lives. They had become an integral part of each other's support system, and their bond had grown stronger with each passing day. Their shared experiences, mutual support, and genuine affection had transformed their friendship into something truly special.

Looking back, both Arhaan and Alankrita recognized the profound impact their friendship had on their lives. They had grown together, supported each other through challenges, and celebrated each other's successes. Their friendship was a testament to the power of connection and the positive influence it could have on one's life.

As they prepared to move forward into the next phase of their lives, Arhaan and Alankrita were excited about the future and the possibilities it held. They knew that their friendship would continue to be a source of strength and support, no matter where life took them. Their bond had been forged through shared experiences, mutual respect, and genuine affection, and it was a connection they cherished deeply.

In the end, Arhaan and Alankrita's friendship was a beautiful example of how meaningful relationships can shape our lives. It had brought them joy, growth, and a sense of belonging, and it was a reminder of the incredible impact that a strong friendship can have. As they looked ahead to the future, they knew that their bond would remain a cherished part of their lives, and they were grateful for the friendship they had built together.

Chapter 7

The Evolution of Emotions: Love Unspoken

As the weeks and months passed, Arhaan's relationship with Alankrita evolved from a casual friendship to a profound and intricate emotional connection. The love he felt for Alankrita was both a source of immense joy and a source of internal conflict, as he struggled to reconcile his feelings with the desire to maintain their friendship.

Arhaan's feelings for Alankrita grew more intense as their friendship deepened. Their interactions, once simple and friendly, began to carry a weight of unspoken affection. Every shared moment became imbued with a new layer of meaning. Arhaan found himself increasingly captivated by Alankrita's presence, the way she spoke, and the way she made him feel valued and understood.

One of the most poignant moments in their evolving relationship was during a school festival. Arhaan and Alankrita had volunteered together for a community service project. They spent the day working side by side, organizing events for younger students and helping to set up decorations. As they worked, their conversation flowed effortlessly, punctuated by shared laughter and occasional, meaningful silences. Arhaan noticed how easily Alankrita connected with everyone around her, and he was struck by her natural ability to lead and inspire.

While they were taking a break, Alankrita spoke passionately about her future aspirations and the causes she cared about. Her idealism and determination were infectious, and Arhaan was deeply moved by her commitment to making a difference. He realized that his admiration for her went beyond mere friendship—it was a profound respect and affection that he could no longer ignore.

Arhaan's feelings were further complicated by moments of vulnerability he experienced with Alankrita. During a particularly stressful period of exams, Arhaan found himself struggling with anxiety and self-doubt. Alankrita, sensing his distress, took it upon herself to provide support. She spent hours helping him study, offering encouragement, and sharing coping strategies. Her empathy and understanding during this time made Arhaan's affection for her grow even stronger. He began to see her not only as a friend but as someone who had a significant impact on his life and well-being.

Despite the deepening of his feelings, Arhaan chose to keep his emotions hidden. The fear of disrupting their friendship and the uncertainty of Alankrita's feelings held him back from confessing his love. Arhaan was acutely aware of the delicate balance between their friendship and his burgeoning emotions. He valued their bond too much to risk it by introducing romantic tension.

Arhaan's internal struggle was marked by moments of introspection and emotional turmoil. He often found himself daydreaming about scenarios where he could express his feelings without jeopardizing their friendship. He would replay conversations in his mind, imagining how he might confess his love and how

Alankrita might respond. These fantasies, while comforting, also added to his internal conflict.

The emotional burden of unspoken love affected Arhaan's daily life. His mood oscillated between elation and melancholy, depending on his interactions with Alankrita. A simple gesture, like a touch on the arm or a shared glance, could uplift his spirits or leave him longing for something more. He became more attuned to the subtleties of their interactions, seeking signs that might indicate whether Alankrita felt the same way.

Arhaan's friends noticed the changes in him. They observed his preoccupation and the occasional wistful look in his eyes. While they were curious, Arhaan chose to keep his feelings private, opting to confide only in his journal. His journal became a sanctuary where he poured out his thoughts and emotions, attempting to make sense of his feelings and the complex dynamics of his relationship with Alankrita.

Arhaan's unspoken love for Alankrita had a significant impact on various aspects of his life. On one hand, it motivated him to strive for personal growth and self-improvement. He became more focused on his studies and extracurricular activities, driven by a desire to become someone who could make a positive impact. His commitment to excellence was fueled by the hope that, one day, he might be worthy of Alankrita's admiration.

His dedication to his goals was evident in his achievements. Arhaan participated in music competitions, excelled in academic subjects, and took on leadership roles in school activities. He pushed himself to new heights, driven by a sense of purpose and the hope that his efforts would lead to personal fulfillment and growth.

On the other hand, the emotional weight of unspoken love also created moments of inner conflict and doubt. Arhaan often grappled with questions about his future and whether he would ever find the courage to express his feelings. He wondered if he would ever have the opportunity to share his love with Alankrita or if he would continue to live with the uncertainty of what might have been.

Arhaan's emotional journey was also marked by moments of profound introspection. He spent time reflecting on the nature of love and friendship, questioning what it meant to truly care for someone. His feelings for Alankrita prompted him to explore deeper philosophical questions about the nature of relationships and the sacrifices one makes for love.

The turning point in Arhaan's emotional journey came as he approached the end of the school year. The prospect of parting ways and facing new challenges made him realize the urgency of his situation. He understood that the time had come to confront his feelings and decide whether to express his love or continue to live with the unspoken truth.

As the end of the school year approached, Arhaan felt a growing sense of urgency. He knew that he needed to make a decision about his future and his feelings for Alankrita. The prospect of leaving behind their familiar environment and facing new opportunities added a sense of finality to his emotions. He felt a heightened sense of both hope and apprehension as he prepared for what lay ahead.

The decision to confess his feelings was not one that Arhaan took lightly. He weighed the potential outcomes, considering both the possibility of a positive response and the risk of rejection. Ultimately, he decided that he needed to be true to himself and to Alankrita. He wanted to express his love, even if it meant facing the possibility of losing their friendship.

Arhaan's journey of unspoken love was characterized by a blend of joy, pain, and introspection. His feelings for Alankrita were a source of profound inspiration and motivation, driving him to become a better person. At the same time, the emotional burden of keeping his love hidden created moments of inner conflict and doubt. As he approached the end of the school year, Arhaan faced a pivotal moment in his life, one that would determine the course of his future and the fate of his relationship with Alankrita.

Chapter 8

The Final Test: Confidence in Growth

As the school year reached its final stretch, the anticipation of the impending final exams created an undercurrent of tension throughout the school. The weeks leading up to the exams were marked by a palpable shift in the atmosphere. The usual lively chatter in the hallways and classrooms gave way to a more subdued, focused environment. The once casual interactions among students became less frequent as they hunkered down for the intense period of study and preparation.

Arhaan had experienced a significant transformation over the past year. His academic performance, once average, had seen a marked improvement thanks to the dedicated support of Alankrita. This period of change was characterized by a rigorous study routine, a profound shift in his approach to learning, and an emerging sense of confidence that contrasted sharply with his earlier uncertainties.

The final exam preparations began in earnest several weeks before the actual test dates. For Arhaan, this meant adopting a disciplined study schedule that was both demanding and rigorous. Each day was structured with precision, beginning early in the morning and extending late into the night. The routine was meticulously planned, encompassing various subjects and a wide range of topics that needed to be reviewed.

Arhaan's mornings started with a review of the material covered the previous day. He would sit at his study desk, surrounded by an array of textbooks, notes, and past papers. His study sessions were characterized by an intense focus, with Arhaan meticulously going through each topic, taking notes, and practicing problems. His approach was systematic, breaking down complex subjects into manageable chunks and tackling them one by one.

During the afternoons, Arhaan would engage in practice tests and mock exams. These sessions were designed to simulate the actual exam environment, helping him to build confidence and manage time effectively. He would time himself while answering questions, mimicking the conditions he would face on the exam day. This practice was crucial in helping him gauge his progress and identify areas that needed further attention.

The evenings were reserved for group study sessions with Alankrita. These sessions were a blend of collaborative learning and mutual support. Alankrita, with her exceptional academic skills and understanding, provided invaluable assistance. They would discuss difficult topics, solve problems together, and clarify doubts. Alankrita's ability to explain complex concepts in a simple and comprehensible manner was a significant factor in Arhaan's academic improvement.

Alankrita's role in Arhaan's preparation was more than just that of a study partner. She had become a mentor, a source of inspiration, and a pillar of support. Her dedication to helping Arhaan extended beyond academic assistance; it also included emotional encouragement. Her belief in his potential and her consistent encouragement played a critical role in shaping Arhaan's confidence.

Alankrita's presence during study sessions was a calming influence. Her methodical approach to learning and her unwavering focus provided a model for Arhaan to emulate. She was meticulous in her preparations, and her own academic performance was a testament to her dedication. This made her advice and guidance all the more impactful.

The dynamic between Arhaan and Alankrita during their study sessions was one of mutual respect and camaraderie. Their interactions were marked by a sense of partnership and shared goals. Alankrita's support was not limited to academics; she also provided moral support, helping Arhaan to navigate the stress and pressure that came with the final exams.

As the exam dates approached, the entire school environment was saturated with a sense of anticipation and anxiety. Students were seen huddled together in study groups, poring over textbooks and exchanging notes. The library, which was normally a quiet refuge, had become a bustling hub of activity. The air was thick with the smell of paper and the sounds of quiet murmurs as students prepared for the exams.

Arhaan observed the varied responses of his peers as they prepared for the exams. Some students were visibly anxious, their faces marked with worry and their actions reflecting a sense of urgency. They were often seen fretting over their study materials or engaging in last-minute cramming sessions. Others exhibited a more confident demeanor, reflecting a sense of readiness and self-assuredness. This spectrum of reactions was a reminder of the diverse approaches students had towards their academic challenges.

Arhaan, however, felt a calm sense of confidence as the exam dates drew near. The rigorous preparation and the support he had received from Alankrita had instilled in him a sense of readiness. He approached the exams with a mindset that was both focused and optimistic. The confidence he had gained from his preparation was a source of strength, enabling him to manage the stress and anxiety that accompanied the exam period.

The day of the first final exam arrived, and with it came a mixture of excitement and nervousness. The school was bustling with activity as students arrived, each carrying their own set of exam materials and anxieties. The corridors, usually filled with casual conversation, were now filled with a subdued, tense energy. Students exchanged last-minute study tips and words of encouragement, their faces reflecting the seriousness of the occasion.

Arhaan arrived at the exam hall, feeling a surge of nervous energy. The large room, lined with rows of desks, was a stark contrast to the familiar classroom setting. The air was filled with the scent of paper and the sound of shuffling feet as students took their seats. Arhaan took a deep breath, focusing on the preparation that had brought him to this point.

As the exam papers were distributed, a hush fell over the room. Arhaan opened his paper and began to read through the questions. His mind raced as he recalled the material he had studied, formulating his responses with a sense of purpose. The hours passed swiftly as he immersed himself in the exam, his confidence evident in the way he tackled each question.

The final exam was a culmination of the hard work and preparation that Arhaan had invested over the year. His responses reflected his improved understanding of the subjects and his ability to apply knowledge effectively. The sense of accomplishment he felt upon completing the exam was a testament to the progress he had made.

The final exam period was a significant milestone in Arhaan's academic journey. It represented the culmination of his efforts and the transformation he had undergone over the past year. The preparation, the support from Alankrita, and the personal growth he had experienced all converged during this critical period.

Arhaan's approach to the final exams was marked by a blend of confidence and dedication, reflecting the impact of his hard work and the guidance he had received. The experience of preparing for and taking the exams was a testament to his growth and development, setting the stage for the next chapter in his life.

Chapter 9

Bittersweet Farewell: The Last Day of School

The final exams had concluded, marking the end of an intense academic journey for Arhaan and his classmates. The last bell had rung, signaling not only the end of exams but also the end of their time together at school. The campus, once a vibrant hub of activity and youthful exuberance, now seemed to echo with a bittersweet silence. As students packed their bags, the air was thick with a mixture of relief, excitement, and melancholy.

For many, this was a moment of joy and liberation. The pressure of exams was over, and summer lay ahead like a blank canvas. Friends exchanged hugs, high-fives, and promises to stay in touch. Laughter and chatter filled the air as students reminisced about their shared experiences and celebrated their achievements. It was a day marked by smiles and farewells, but for Arhaan, it was a day tinged with a deeper, more complex set of emotions.

Arhaan stood at the edge of the schoolyard, watching as his classmates interacted with a sense of carefree joy. To an outsider, he might have seemed detached, his usual enthusiasm subdued. Inside, however, a storm of emotions raged. He was grateful that the exams were over, yet his heart was weighed down by the realization that this day might be the last time he would see Alankrita.

Throughout the year, Alankrita had become more than just a friend to Arhaan. She had been his guide, his confidant, and a source of unwavering support. Their bond had deepened over time, and now, as the school year drew to a close, the prospect of parting ways filled him with a profound sense of loss.

Arhaan tried to focus on the positive aspects of the day. He had performed well in his exams, a feat that had seemed improbable at the beginning of the year. His hard work had paid off, and he felt a sense of accomplishment and relief. Yet, the looming reality of saying goodbye to Alankrita cast a shadow over his joy.

As the day wore on, students began to drift out of the

school, some heading straight for summer plans while others lingered to say their goodbyes. Arhaan searched for Alankrita, feeling a mixture of urgency and anxiety. The thought of not having a final, meaningful conversation with her was unbearable.

He spotted her standing near the school gate, surrounded by a group of friends. Alankrita was radiant as ever, her fair skin glowing in the afternoon sun, her long black hair cascading over her shoulders. She was animatedly chatting with her friends, her laughter ringing out like a sweet melody. Despite the general cheerfulness, Arhaan noticed a wistful look in her eyes, a subtle indication that she, too, was feeling the weight of the moment.

Taking a deep breath, Arhaan approached her. His heart pounded in his chest, and he could feel a lump forming in his throat. He had rehearsed what he wanted to say, but in the face of the reality of their separation, the words seemed to escape him.

"Hey, Alankrita," he said, his voice betraying a hint of nervousness.

Alankrita turned towards him, her eyes brightening with a warm smile. "Hey, Arhaan! You finally made it over here. I thought you'd be busy celebrating with everyone."

Arhaan managed a weak smile. "I was just... trying to find the right moment. I wanted to talk to you before we all went our separate ways."

Alankrita's smile softened, and she nodded, her gaze steady. "Of course. What's on your mind?"

Arhaan hesitated, struggling to articulate the jumble of emotions inside him. He looked around, noticing the bustling activity around them, and decided that they needed a quieter place to talk. "Let's go for a walk," he suggested. "There's something I want to say, and I'd rather not do it here with everyone around."

Alankrita agreed, and they walked together to a nearby park, a place they had often visited during their school days. The park was peaceful, a stark contrast to the lively atmosphere of the schoolyard. They found a bench under a large oak tree and sat down, the quiet ambiance providing a backdrop for their conversation.

Sitting beside her, Arhaan felt a mixture of comfort and sadness. He glanced at Alankrita, noting how serene she looked. The golden light of the setting sun cast a warm glow on her face, accentuating her features and adding an ethereal quality to the moment.

"Alankrita," he began, his voice trembling slightly, "this year has been... incredible. I don't know where to start. You've been such an important part of it for me."

Alankrita looked at him, her expression attentive and gentle. "You've been an important part of my year too, Arhaan. We've shared so many experiences, and I'm really grateful for your friendship."

Arhaan swallowed hard, the lump in his throat growing. "I... I wanted to thank you for everything. For helping me with my studies, for always being there. I don't know how I would have gotten through this year without you."

Alankrita smiled, a touch of sadness in her eyes. "You would have done great on your own, Arhaan. You're smart and capable. But I'm glad I could be there for you."

There was a brief pause as Arhaan gathered his thoughts. "It's just... it's hard to say goodbye. I know we're all moving on, and things will change, but..."

Alankrita reached out and touched his hand gently. "I know it's hard. Change is never easy, but it's a part of life. We have our memories, and we'll always have those."

Arhaan's eyes met hers, and he could see the sincerity in her gaze. "I wish things didn't have to change. I wish we could stay like this forever."

Alankrita's smile was both bittersweet and understanding. "We can't stay the same forever. But we can cherish the moments we've had and look forward to the new experiences ahead. Life goes on, and we'll find new paths."

As they sat together, the sun began to dip below the horizon, casting long shadows across the park. The beauty of the evening was a stark contrast to the turmoil Arhaan felt inside. He could sense the finality of the moment, the realization that this was truly the end of an era for them.

With the sky turning a soft shade of pink and orange, Arhaan and Alankrita stood up from the bench. They walked slowly back towards the school, their footsteps echoing the weight of the moment. As they reached the school gate, the crowd of students had thinned, and the air was filled with a quiet, reflective atmosphere.

Arhaan took a deep breath, his heart heavy with the knowledge that this was their final farewell. He turned to Alankrita, his voice barely above a whisper. "Thank you, Alankrita. For everything. I'll always remember this year and how much you've meant to me."

Alankrita's eyes were filled with tears, but her smile remained. "Thank you, Arhaan. I'll remember it too. You've been a wonderful friend, and I wish you all the best for the future."

They stood there for a moment, the world around them fading into the background. The finality of their farewell was underscored by the gentle evening breeze and the soft sounds of the park.

Finally, Arhaan hugged Alankrita, his emotions spilling over. The embrace was tender and heartfelt, a silent acknowledgment of their shared bond and the pain of parting. As they pulled away, Arhaan felt a tear roll down his cheek. Alankrita, too, had tears in her eyes, but she managed to smile through them.

"Goodbye, Alankrita," Arhaan said softly.

"Goodbye, Arhaan," Alankrita replied, her voice filled with warmth and affection.

With one last look, they parted ways. Arhaan watched as Alankrita walked away, her figure gradually disappearing into the distance. The weight of their farewell lingered with him, a reminder of the deep connection they had shared and the inevitability of change.

As Arhaan left the school grounds, he reflected on the emotional complexity of the day. He felt a mixture of relief and sadness, the joy of completing his exams overshadowed by the pain of saying goodbye to someone who had become so important to him.

The memories of his time with Alankrita would remain a cherished part of his life. Despite the sorrow of their parting, he found solace in the knowledge that their friendship had been genuine and meaningful. The experiences they had shared and the bond they had formed were invaluable, and he would carry those memories with him as he moved forward into the next chapter of his life.

The last day of school was a poignant reminder of the transient nature of life. It was a day of endings and new beginnings, a moment when the past and the future converged. Arhaan's farewell to Alankrita was both a culmination of their shared experiences and a step towards new opportunities and challenges.

As he walked away from the school, Arhaan felt a renewed sense of purpose. The end of the school year marked the beginning of a new journey, one that would be shaped by the lessons he had learned and the friendships he had forged. The memories of Alankrita would remain a source of inspiration and strength as he faced the future with hope and determination.

Chapter 10

A Heart's Confession: Love Amidst Ambition

As the autumn leaves began to fall, marking the passage of time since the end of school, Arhaan found himself in the midst of a pivotal moment in his life. The summer break had given way to a new routine cantered around his preparation for engineering entrance exams. Each day was a meticulously planned sequence of study sessions, practice tests, and review meetings with tutors. The weight of his ambition to secure a place in a prestigious engineering college was ever-present, shaping his daily life and driving his every action.

Arhaan's room had transformed into a study haven, filled with textbooks, notes, and reference materials. The once neat and orderly space now bore the marks of his academic pursuit—a testament to the countless hours he had dedicated to his studies. The walls were adorned with motivational quotes and diagrams, while the desk was cluttered with papers, pens, and highlighters. It was a place where determination and focus converged, providing a refuge from the chaos of his inner emotional conflict.

Despite the structure and discipline that his studies provided, Arhaan was grappling with an emotional turmoil that refused to be silenced. The past few months had been a blend of rigorous academic work and an internal battle that was both intense and exhausting. His feelings for Alankrita, which had started as a deep admiration and affection, had grown into something more profound—a love that he could no longer ignore.

The memories of their time together lingered in his mind, often resurfacing during moments of quiet reflection. The laughter they shared, the conversations that flowed effortlessly, and the comfort of their friendship were all reminders of the bond they once had. Arhaan found himself caught in a cycle of longing and regret, unable to fully immerse himself in his studies without the constant reminder of what he had left unsaid.

As he navigated the complexities of his preparation, the pressure to succeed academically was compounded by the weight of his unspoken feelings. The duality of his life—one driven by ambition and the other by love—created a dissonance that was difficult to reconcile. Each day brought a new set of challenges and triumphs in his academic pursuits, but the emotional unrest remained a constant undercurrent, influencing his mood and mindset.

Arhaan's struggle to maintain focus on his studies was evident in the way he approached his daily routine. The rigorous demands of preparing for the entrance exams required a level of concentration and dedication that often felt at odds with the emotional distractions he faced. While he was diligent in his study sessions, he frequently found his thoughts drifting to Alankrita— wondering how she was doing, what she was thinking, and how she might react to his feelings if he were to express them.

His interactions with friends and family were marked by a reserved demeanor, as he struggled to mask his internal conflict. Conversations with his parents and peers often revolved around his academic progress, but he remained guarded when it came to discussing his personal life. The contrast between his outward appearance of composure and the inner chaos was a source of frustration, leaving him feeling isolated and misunderstood.

Despite his best efforts to stay focused, there were moments when the emotional strain of his unspoken love became overwhelming. The pressure of the entrance exams, combined with the weight of his feelings, created a sense of urgency that he could no longer ignore. Arhaan was caught in a cycle of trying to balance his academic goals with the emotional turmoil that had become an integral part of his life.

The turning point came one evening after an intense study session. Arhaan was seated at his desk, surrounded by textbooks and notes, when he felt a profound sense of weariness. The combination of academic pressure and emotional strain had reached a peak, and he realized that he could no longer continue to suppress his feelings without addressing them.

He leaned back in his chair, staring at the ceiling as he contemplated the decision that lay before him. The realization that he needed to confront his feelings head-on was both liberating and daunting. Arhaan understood that this was not just about expressing his emotions but about finding closure and clarity in a situation that had been clouded by uncertainty.

The decision to confess his feelings to Alankrita was driven by a need for resolution—a desire to move forward with a sense of honesty and authenticity. He recognized that his feelings for her had become a significant part of his life, influencing his thoughts and actions. The prospect of confessing his love was accompanied by a mixture of fear and hope, as he grappled with the potential outcomes and their implications for his future.

The decision to confess was not made lightly. Arhaan spent several days reflecting on the implications of his choice, considering how it would affect both his own emotional well-being and his relationship with

Alankrita. The prospect of exposing his vulnerability and facing the possibility of rejection was a daunting challenge, but he felt that it was a necessary step in his journey.

Arhaan's emotions were a complex mix of anticipation, apprehension, and hope. He was acutely aware of the risks involved, including the possibility of disrupting the friendship that had become a source of strength and support. However, the emotional burden of keeping his feelings concealed had become too great to bear. The confession was not just about revealing his love but also about finding a path forward that allowed him to be true to himself.

In the days leading up to the confession, Arhaan found himself oscillating between moments of resolve and doubt. He would imagine various scenarios, considering how Alankrita might respond and what it would mean for their future. The emotional weight of his decision was both a source of motivation and a cause of anxiety, making each day a blend of anticipation and uncertainty.

With the decision made, Arhaan prepared himself for the next steps. He knew that he needed to approach the confession with sincerity and respect, acknowledging the significance of the moment and the potential impact on their relationship. The process of preparing for his confession was an integral part of his emotional journey, as he sought to find the right balance between honesty and sensitivity.

Arhaan's preparation involved not only reflecting on his feelings but also considering how to communicate them effectively. He wanted to ensure that his message conveyed the depth of his emotions while also respecting Alankrita's perspective and feelings. The process of drafting and revising his thoughts was an important step in finding the right words and approach.

As the entrance exams approached, Arhaan was faced with the challenge of balancing his academic commitments with his emotional resolution. The final weeks of preparation were marked by a heightened sense of urgency, as he worked to complete his studies and finalize his plans for the confession. The emotional journey had been both arduous and transformative, shaping his approach to the upcoming exams and his interaction with Alankrita.

As Arhaan prepared to confess his feelings to Alankrita, he was acutely aware of the significance of the moment. The journey had been a complex interplay of ambition, emotion, and personal growth, leading him to a point of emotional clarity and resolution. The decision to express his feelings was not just about seeking closure but about embracing his truth and finding a path forward.

In the days that followed, Arhaan remained focused on his studies while also preparing for the conversation that lay ahead. The process of confronting his feelings and taking the step to confess was a testament to his growth and determination. As he approached the final stretch of his preparation for the engineering entrance exams, he was filled with a sense of purpose and resolve, ready to face whatever the future held.

Chapter 11

The Digital Confession: A Message Sent

In the era of technological advancement, social media had become a cornerstone of communication. Platforms like Profileblock had revolutionized the way people connected, allowing for instantaneous sharing of thoughts, emotions, and updates. This digital landscape was a natural extension of daily life, and it had become the primary means through which people maintained their relationships and expressed their feelings.

For Arhaan, Profileblock was more than just a social media platform; it was a reflection of his connections and interactions. It had become a familiar space where he navigated his social world, keeping in touch with friends and acquaintances, and sharing glimpses of his life.

Arhaan and Alankrita had been connected on Profileblock for a while. Their connection was a product of their shared social circle and the natural flow of digital interactions. Their exchanges had mostly been casual, with likes, comments, and occasional messages. This connection, though relatively passive, had become an important part of their digital presence.

The familiarity of Profileblock made it a logical choice for Arhaan when he decided to express his feelings. It was a space where he had interacted with Alankrita before, and it provided a sense of comfort and accessibility. Despite the nature of their interactions being mostly superficial, the platform represented a bridge between their worlds—a space where their virtual connection could potentially evolve into something more meaningful.

As Arhaan's feelings for Alankrita deepened, he faced a pivotal decision. The need to articulate his emotions had become increasingly urgent. The digital age had made communication easier, but it also presented its own set of challenges. The immediacy and convenience of social media seemed like the right avenue for Arhaan to convey his feelings, despite its limitations.

The choice of using Profileblock for his confession was influenced by its familiarity and the sense of comfort it offered. It was a space where he had previously interacted with Alankrita, making it a natural platform for his message. The decision to use a digital medium was both practical and symbolic, reflecting the reality of their modern, interconnected lives.

Arhaan's process of drafting the message was a blend of emotional intensity and careful consideration. He wanted to ensure that his words were heartfelt and sincere, capturing the depth of his feelings while being mindful of Alankrita's potential reaction. The digital nature of the message required him to be clear and concise, avoiding any potential misinterpretations that could arise from text-based communication.

The drafting process involved several revisions. Arhaan reflected on his emotions, trying to encapsulate his feelings in a way that was genuine and respectful. He considered the moments they had shared, the reasons for his affection, and the impact his message might have. The goal was to express his emotions honestly without overwhelming Alankrita or putting undue pressure on her.

Once Arhaan was satisfied with the content of his message, he faced the crucial moment of sending it. The act of clicking the "send" button was both exhilarating and nerve-wracking. It was a step into the unknown, a moment that would potentially alter the dynamics of his relationship with Alankrita.

As he prepared to send the message, Arhaan's thoughts were a whirlwind of anticipation and anxiety. The message was a culmination of his emotional journey and a leap into uncertainty. The digital platform offered a sense of distance, but it also lacked the personal touch of face-to-face communication. Nevertheless, it was the medium through which Arhaan chose to express his feelings.

With a deep breath and a mix of hope and trepidation, Arhaan clicked the "send" button. The message was now in Alankrita's digital inbox, awaiting her attention. The immediate act of sending it was a release of tension, but it also marked the beginning of a new phase of uncertainty.

In the days that followed, Arhaan found himself in a state of heightened anticipation. The digital age had introduced a new layer of immediacy to communication, and the waiting period was filled with a blend of hope and nervousness. Every notification on his phone carried the possibility of a response, and Arhaan's attention was constantly drawn to the screen, hoping for a sign from Alankrita.

During this time, Arhaan's thoughts were consumed by the message he had sent. He wondered how Alankrita would react and whether his words had conveyed his feelings accurately. The waiting period was marked by a mix of excitement and anxiety, as Arhaan grappled with the uncertainty of the outcome.

The choice to use social media for his confession had significant implications. While it provided a convenient and immediate platform for communication, it also came with limitations. The digital nature of the message meant that it lacked the nuances of face-to-face interaction, and the immediate feedback that could be obtained from personal conversations was absent.

Arhaan realized that social media, despite its advantages, could not fully capture the depth of human emotions. The limitations of text-based communication became apparent as he awaited Alankrita's response. The absence of tone, body language, and immediate feedback made the process of waiting for a response more challenging.

As Arhaan awaited Alankrita's response, he reflected on the experience of using social media for such a personal revelation. The digital medium, while convenient, had its own set of challenges. Arhaan acknowledged that the nature of social media could sometimes complicate the expression of genuine emotions.

The process of sending the message had been a significant step in Arhaan's emotional journey. It represented a moment of vulnerability and courage, and it marked a turning point in his relationship with Alankrita. The digital confession had set in motion a series of events that would shape the future of their connection.

As Arhaan continued to navigate the aftermath of his confession, he focused on moving forward with his life. The experience had been a catalyst for personal growth and reflection. While the outcome of his message remained uncertain, Arhaan remained committed to his goals and aspirations.

The digital confession had been a significant step in Arhaan's journey of self-expression and emotional discovery. It highlighted the complexities of modern communication and the challenges of navigating relationships in the digital age. Despite the uncertainties, Arhaan's experience served as a valuable lesson in resilience and the importance of honest communication.

In the weeks that followed, Arhaan continued to pursue his academic and personal goals. The impact of his confession became a part of his life experience, shaping his perspective on relationships and communication. While the outcome of his message

was not yet clear, Arhaan's commitment to his goals
and his resilience in the face of uncertainty remained
unwavering.

Chapter 12

Silence Speaks: Moving Forward

The digital landscape was a vast expanse, filled with endless possibilities for connection and communication. Yet, in its vastness, it could also be a place of profound silence and uncertainty. For Arhaan, this silence became a backdrop for his emotional turbulence and introspection following his heartfelt confession to Alankrita.

In the days following Arhaan's confession to Alankrita on Profileblock, he found himself enveloped in a growing sense of unease. The message he had sent, filled with his deepest emotions, had not been responded to. This absence of reply was not just a lack of communication—it was a silence that spoke volumes, a void that seemed to echo his unspoken fears and doubts.

Arhaan's anticipation had been palpable. Each notification on his phone, each ping of a message, had been met with a flutter of hope. But as days turned into weeks, the anticipated reply never arrived. The silence was heavy, almost oppressive, as if it was pressing down on him from all sides, suffocating him with its weight.

The lack of response from Alankrita was more than just a minor setback; it was an emotional blow. Arhaan had invested his feelings into that message, and the silence that followed felt like a rejection of those emotions. He experienced a range of emotions, from confusion to disappointment, anger to sadness. It was as if his heart was caught in a whirlwind of conflicting feelings, each one intensifying the others.

The anger Arhaan felt was directed both at himself and at the situation. He was angry at himself for choosing a method of communication that might not have been the most effective. The frustration was compounded by the fact that he had opened up in a way that left him feeling vulnerable and exposed. The absence of a reply felt like a personal affront, a dismissal of the genuine feelings he had shared.

Yet, despite his anger, there was a part of Arhaan that

understood the nature of the situation. Deep down, he knew that his confession, despite its sincerity, might not have been received in the way he had hoped. The digital medium had its limitations, and the reality of his feelings might not have translated well through a screen.

Arhaan's reflection on his actions revealed a deeper understanding of his own motivations and the nature of his emotions. He recognized that his decision to confess via social media was influenced by his own sense of urgency and the constraints of their digital age. While it had seemed like a straightforward way to communicate his feelings, the outcome had shown him the limitations and potential pitfalls of such an approach.

The decision to confess was driven by his desire to be honest and transparent about his feelings. However, the lack of response had made him question whether he had chosen the right path. The silence forced him to confront the possibility that his feelings might not have been reciprocated, or that the medium of communication might have been a barrier to understanding.

Arhaan's internal dialogue was filled with a mix of regret and acceptance. He pondered whether he should have approached the situation differently—perhaps through a more personal or direct method. The reflection was a painful yet necessary process, helping him to come to terms with the outcome and the limitations of his chosen method.

Despite the emotional turmoil, Arhaan understood that he needed to move forward. The period of silence had been a catalyst for personal growth and a reevaluation of his priorities. He realized that dwelling on the lack of response would only hold him back from pursuing his goals and aspirations.

With a renewed sense of determination, Arhaan shifted his focus to his ambitions. He channeled his energy into his studies and his preparation for the engineering entrance exams. The silence from Alankrita, though painful, became a catalyst for his growth, pushing him to redirect his energy towards his personal and professional goals.

Arhaan's newfound focus was evident in his daily routine. He dedicated himself to his studies with a vigor that had previously been overshadowed by his emotional preoccupations. The drive to succeed became a powerful force, propelling him forward and giving him a sense of purpose.

The period following his confession was marked by a period of intense self-improvement and dedication. Arhaan immersed himself in his studies, striving to excel in his academic pursuits. His commitment to his goals was unwavering, and he found solace in the progress he was making.

The silence from Alankrita became a part of his past, a chapter that had closed but left behind valuable lessons. Arhaan embraced his ambition with a renewed sense of purpose. The drive to achieve something greater became his primary focus, and he was determined to make the most of the opportunities before him.

Arhaan's academic achievements and his progress towards his goals were a testament to his resilience and determination. The pain of unrequited feelings had been transformed into a powerful motivator, fuelling his quest for success and fulfilment.

Arhaan's journey through this challenging period taught him important lessons about strength and resilience. The emotional impact of Alankrita's silence had been profound, but it had also revealed his capacity to endure and grow. The experience highlighted his ability to confront adversity and emerge stronger from it.

The absence of a reply, while disheartening, had become a catalyst for personal growth. Arhaan's ability to move forward and channel his energy into his ambitions was a testament to his character and his determination. The experience had been a test of his resilience, and he had come through it with a renewed sense of purpose.

As Arhaan continued on his path, the lessons from this experience remained with him. The silence from

Alankrita had been a painful chapter, but it had also been a formative one. Arhaan's journey was now marked by a deeper understanding of himself and his goals.

The road ahead was filled with opportunities and challenges, and Arhaan approached it with a sense of optimism and determination. The experience had shaped his perspective, helping him to appreciate the importance of perseverance and the value of focusing on one's aspirations.

Arhaan's commitment to his goals remained steadfast. The experience of dealing with unrequited feelings and navigating the complexities of digital communication had made him more aware of the intricacies of relationships and personal growth. As he moved forward, he carried with him the lessons learned and the strength gained from this challenging period.

Chapter 13

The Silent Message: An Echo from the Past

In the ever-evolving landscape of digital communication, a simple message can carry profound significance. For Arhaan, the arrival of a text message from Alankrita after several months of silence marked a moment of unexpected and complex emotions. It was a digital echo from the past, stirring up a mixture of curiosity, confusion, and nostalgia.

Arhaan was engrossed in his studies, his days marked by a rigorous routine of preparation for the engineering entrance exams. His world had been a blur of textbooks, notes, and practice tests. Amidst this academic whirlwind, a notification on his phone pierced through his concentration. It was a message from Alankrita—"Hi Arhaan."

The simplicity of the message was stark against the backdrop of the silence that had followed his confession months earlier. The message was brief, yet it held a weight of its own. The lack of context and the abruptness of the greeting left Arhaan in a state of confusion. He wondered about the meaning behind this sudden outreach and the intentions that might lie behind it.

Arhaan's initial reaction was one of surprise. He had not anticipated any further communication from Alankrita, especially given the absence of a response to his previous confession. The message seemed out of place, an anomaly in the routine he had become accustomed to. It was a digital remnant from a time that seemed to belong to a different chapter of his life.

He pondered over the message, weighing its significance. Was it an attempt to reconnect, or merely a casual greeting with no deeper meaning? The message lacked substance, making it difficult to gauge its true intent. Arhaan found himself caught between a desire to respond and an uncertainty about how to approach the situation.

To fully understand Arhaan's reaction, it was essential to consider the context of the silence that had preceded the message. The period of silence had been a time of introspection and growth for Arhaan. The lack of response to his confession had been a painful yet formative experience, shaping his approach to relationships and communication.

During these months, Arhaan had channelled his energy into his studies and personal development. He had embraced his ambitions with a newfound focus, using the silence as a catalyst for his growth. The unexpected message from Alankrita came at a time when he was deeply immersed in his academic pursuits, making it all the more jarring.

The message from Alankrita stirred a complex mix of emotions within Arhaan. There was a sense of nostalgia, a reminder of the connection they once shared. It was a glimpse into the past, a reminder of the friendship that had flourished before the silence had set in. The simplicity of the message contrasted sharply with the depth of the feelings that had once been part of their interactions.

At the same time, there was a lingering sense of uncertainty. The lack of a follow-up to the initial message left Arhaan grappling with unanswered questions. Was there a reason behind the message, or was it a casual attempt at rekindling a connection without any real intent? The ambiguity created a sense of awkwardness, leaving him unsure of how to proceed.

Despite the emotional turmoil stirred by the message, Arhaan decided to take a measured approach. His current focus was on his studies and preparing for his exams, and he was wary of allowing the message to distract him from his goals. He recognized the importance of maintaining his academic momentum and chose to prioritize his studies over immediate responses to the message.

The decision to delay responding was not made lightly. Arhaan wanted to ensure that his response, if and when it came, was thoughtful and considered. He was mindful of the fact that any reply might reopen old wounds or lead to further complications, and he wanted to avoid making hasty decisions driven by emotional impulses.

Arhaan's commitment to his studies provided a sense of stability and purpose during this period. The exams were approaching, and his preparation was intense. The discipline and focus required for his academic endeavours helped him navigate the emotional complexities stirred by the message from Alankrita.

The message, while significant, was ultimately a small part of his broader journey. Arhaan's dedication to his goals remained unwavering, and he used his academic pursuits as a means of grounding himself amidst the uncertainty. The rigorous study schedule became a source of comfort, offering a clear sense of direction and purpose.

The unexpected message from Alankrita also had a subtle impact on Arhaan's daily routine. The notification had briefly disrupted his concentration, and the ensuing contemplation about how to respond added an extra layer of complexity to his already busy life. It was a reminder of the emotional landscape he had been navigating, a landscape that now included both past and present elements.

Despite this disruption, Arhaan remained focused on his routine. His study sessions were marked by a renewed sense of determination, and he continued to make progress towards his academic goals. The message from Alankrita was a fleeting but significant event, one that highlighted the intertwining of personal and academic aspects of his life.

As days passed, the initial shock of the message began to fade, but it left behind a lingering sense of reflection. Arhaan found himself contemplating the nature of his relationship with Alankrita and the evolution of their connection over time. The message was a reminder of the complexities of human relationships and the ways in which they can evolve and shift.

The silence that followed the message also prompted Arhaan to reflect on his own journey. The period of separation had been a time of personal growth and self-discovery, and he was now in a different place emotionally. The message served as a reminder of how much he had changed and how his perspective had evolved.

Arhaan's approach to the situation involved waiting and observing. He was mindful of the fact that responding to the message too quickly could lead to further complications. The absence of a follow-up from Alankrita left him in a state of limbo, unsure of whether or not further communication would follow.

The waiting game became a part of Arhaan's routine, a subtle undercurrent to his daily activities. It was a reminder of the unpredictable nature of relationships and the ways in which they can intersect with other aspects of life. The uncertainty surrounding the message was a reflection of the broader uncertainties that often accompany human connections.

In the midst of this emotional and academic landscape, Arhaan began to channel his energy into new avenues. The message from Alankrita, while significant, did not overshadow his commitment to his goals. He used the situation as an opportunity to reaffirm his focus and dedication.

Arhaan's new energy was evident in his academic achievements and his approach to his studies. The message from Alankrita, while a notable event, was integrated into his broader journey of personal growth and ambition. The experience highlighted his ability to navigate complex emotional terrain while maintaining a clear sense of purpose.

Chapter 14

Blocked: The Digital Rejection

Months of relentless effort and dedication had finally paid off for Arhaan. His focus and commitment to his academic pursuits had led him to secure admission in a prestigious college for technical graduation in engineering and design. It was a significant achievement, a milestone that marked the culmination of years of hard work and determination.

The transition from high school to college was a pivotal moment for Arhaan. It represented not just a new academic challenge, but also a fresh chapter in his life. The prestige of the college and the rigorous nature of the program were a testament to his capabilities and perseverance. The prospect of delving into the world of engineering and design was both exhilarating and daunting.

Arhaan's engagement with his studies was total and all-consuming. The demands of his coursework were intense, and he found himself fully immersed in the academic environment. His days were structured around lectures, assignments, projects, and study sessions. The college environment was vibrant and fast-paced, with a constant flow of new information and challenges.

This immersion in his studies left little room for distractions. Social media, which had once been a significant part of his daily routine, took a backseat. Arhaan's focus was on mastering his coursework, collaborating with peers on projects, and adapting to the new academic demands. The once-familiar notifications and updates from social media platforms became background noise as he prioritized his academic responsibilities.

As the first semester came to a close, Arhaan found a moment of respite from his academic obligations. It was a brief pause that allowed him to catch his breath and reflect on his achievements. During this period, he decided to revisit his social media accounts, specifically Profileblock, a platform he had previously been active on but had neglected during his intense study period.

Reinstalling the Profileblock app was a symbolic gesture, a reconnection with a part of his past that had been overshadowed by his current pursuits. Arhaan's intention was to reconnect with old friends, catch up on missed updates, and perhaps relive some of the social interactions that had been part of his life before his focus shifted so dramatically.

Upon logging into Profileblock, Arhaan was met with an unexpected and unsettling revelation. As he navigated through his connections and messages, he noticed that Alankrita had blocked him. The notification was a jarring contrast to the sense of achievement and relief he had felt upon finishing his first semester.

The discovery of being blocked was not just a technical detail; it was an emotional jolt. Alankrita had been a significant part of Arhaan's life, and the abrupt end to their online connection felt like a sudden severing of ties. The block was a stark reminder of the unresolved complexities and emotional turbulence that had marked their past interactions.

The realization that Alankrita had blocked him prompted a wave of emotions for Arhaan. There was a mix of confusion, hurt, and introspection. The block was a silent but powerful statement, one that left Arhaan grappling with questions and uncertainties.

He reflected on their past interactions, trying to understand if there had been any signals or indications that he had missed. The block seemed to erase the possibility of further communication, leaving him with a sense of finality and unresolved feelings. It was a reminder of the distance that had grown between them and the complexity of their previous connection.

The impact of discovering the block was multifaceted. On one hand, it was a personal blow, a reminder of the emotional and relational dynamics that had been part of his life. On the other hand, it was a reminder of how much he had grown and changed since their last interaction.

Arhaan's journey had been marked by significant personal development and academic achievement. The block from Alankrita, while disheartening, did not overshadow the progress he had made. It was a part of his past, a chapter that had its place in his story but did not define his present or future.

Arhaan's experience with social media, and specifically with Profileblock, became a point of reflection. The platform had been a conduit for connections and interactions, but it also highlighted the transient nature of digital relationships. The block was a reminder of how easily connections could be made or severed in the digital age.

As he navigated through the platform, Arhaan considered the role of social media in his life. The initial excitement of reconnecting with old friends and reliving past interactions was overshadowed by the emotional impact of the block. It was a stark reminder of how digital connections could influence real-life emotions and relationships.

Despite the emotional impact of discovering the block, Arhaan chose to focus on his achievements and future prospects. His first semester had been a period of significant growth and accomplishment, and he was determined to continue building on that foundation.

Arhaan's dedication to his studies and his commitment to his goals remained unwavering. The block from Alankrita was a part of his past, but it did not define his future. He channeled his energy into his academic pursuits and continued to make progress in his program. The challenges and triumphs of his college experience became the focus of his attention.

The block from Alankrita also provided Arhaan with a broader perspective on relationships and personal growth. It was a reminder of the complexities of human connections and the ways in which they can evolve over time. The digital world, with its ephemeral nature, contrasted sharply with the tangible achievements and experiences that marked Arhaan's academic journey.

Arhaan's reflection on the block and his experiences with social media led him to appreciate the value of real-life connections and the importance of focusing on his own growth and development. The block was a moment of disruption, but it also served as a catalyst for deeper introspection and a reaffirmation of his commitment to his goals.

The discovery that Alankrita had blocked him on Profileblock was a significant moment in Arhaan's journey. It was an unexpected and emotionally charged experience that highlighted the complexities of relationships and the impact of digital interactions on real-life emotions.

As Arhaan moved forward, he embraced the lessons learned from this experience and continued to focus on his academic and personal growth. The block was a part of his past, but it did not define his future. Arhaan's dedication to his studies and his commitment to his goals remained his primary focus, and he approached the future with a sense of determination and resilience.

Chapter 15

Unspoken Truths: The Unblocking Mystery

The shock of being blocked on Profileblock by Alankrita lingered in Arhaan's mind, casting a shadow over his academic achievements and personal growth. The suddenness of the block, without any apparent reason, left him perplexed and unsettled. Despite his best efforts to move forward, he found himself unable to fully shake off the lingering questions and emotions related to this abrupt severance of their online connection.

As the weeks went by, Arhaan's curiosity about the block grew. He had tried to rationalize it, to focus on his studies and his burgeoning career, but the unanswered questions remained a persistent nagging in the back of his mind. Why had Alankrita blocked him? Was there something he had missed or done wrong? The uncertainty surrounding the situation made it difficult for him to find closure.

In an attempt to gain some clarity, Arhaan decided to

reach out to Rima, a mutual friend who had been close to both him and Alankrita. Rima had always been a bridge between them, and Arhaan hoped that she might provide some insight into the situation. He approached Rima with a sense of cautious optimism, hoping that she might be able to shed some light on the mystery of the block.

When Arhaan contacted Rima, he was careful to phrase his inquiry in a way that was respectful of both her and Alankrita's privacy. He explained his confusion and disappointment over the block and asked if Rima could perhaps talk to Alankrita to understand why this had happened. Arhaan was aware that he was treading on delicate ground, but his desire for closure outweighed his reservations.

Rima, ever the diplomat, agreed to speak with Alankrita on Arhaan's behalf. She understood the emotional weight of the situation and approached the conversation with sensitivity. However, when Rima broached the topic with Alankrita, she was met with a surprising response.

Alankrita was nonchalant about the entire situation. She did not provide Rima with any specific reasons for blocking Arhaan, nor did she offer any explanations or apologies. Her demeanor was calm and detached, as if the block was an inconsequential matter that did not warrant further discussion. This response left Rima in an awkward position, as she was unable to provide Arhaan with any concrete answers.

Shortly after Rima's conversation with Alankrita, Arhaan noticed a change. Alankrita had unblocked him on Profileblock. The timing of this action was curious, as it coincided with the end of Rima's conversation with her. Arhaan was both relieved and confused by this development. The block had been lifted, but the reasons behind it remained elusive.

When Arhaan initiated contact with Alankrita, he was greeted with a tone of normalcy. The conversation began as if nothing had happened, with Alankrita engaging in their usual friendly banter. She seemed to be treating their interaction as if the block had never occurred, which further deepened Arhaan's confusion.

As they chatted, Arhaan was tempted to confront Alankrita about the block. He wanted to understand why it had happened and what had prompted her to reverse her decision. However, Alankrita skillfully avoided addressing the issue directly. Her responses were polite and engaged, but she deflected any inquiries related to the block with ease.

Arhaan's attempts to probe further were met with general responses that did not address the core issue. He found himself caught in a delicate balance between expressing his curiosity and maintaining the flow of the conversation. Despite his internal struggle, he chose to keep the conversation light and amicable, not wanting to jeopardize the fragile peace that had been restored.

The conversation between Arhaan and Alankrita, while friendly, was tinged with an undercurrent of unresolved tension. Arhaan was acutely aware of the unspoken issues that lay between them. The block, while now removed, had left a mark on their relationship. The normalcy of their interaction did not erase the fact that something had been disrupted.

During their conversation, Arhaan noticed that Alankrita was engaging in their usual topics and interests. They discussed their recent experiences, shared updates about their lives, and reminisced about past memories. Despite the warmth of their exchange, the shadow of the block remained a subtle but persistent presence in Arhaan's mind.

As the conversation drew to a close, Arhaan and Alankrita ended on a positive note. They exchanged pleasantries and expressed good wishes for each other's future endeavors. Arhaan was left with a sense of bittersweet relief. The interaction had restored a semblance of normalcy, but the lack of clarity regarding the block left him with unresolved feelings.

Arhaan's decision to move forward without pressing for answers was a conscious one. He recognized that some questions might remain unanswered and that not all issues could be resolved to his satisfaction. The conversation had provided a temporary reprieve from the confusion, but it had not fully addressed the underlying concerns.

The experience of being blocked, and then having the block lifted without explanation, was a significant chapter in Arhaan's journey. It highlighted the complexities of modern relationships and the impact of digital interactions on real-life emotions. The episode served as a reminder of the fragile nature of connections in the digital age and the challenges of navigating interpersonal dynamics in a rapidly evolving world.

Arhaan's interactions with Alankrita, and the subsequent conversation following the unblocking, were reflective of the broader themes of growth and understanding in his life. The process of seeking answers and finding a way to move forward was emblematic of his broader journey toward self-awareness and resilience.

As Arhaan continued with his academic and personal pursuits, he carried the lessons from this experience with him. The block, and the subsequent resolution, became a part of his larger narrative of growth and self-discovery. While the reasons behind the block remained unclear, Arhaan's focus was on embracing the opportunities and challenges that lay ahead.

The unblocking and the conversation with Alankrita were moments of reflection and adjustment. They were a reminder of the importance of resilience and the ability to navigate complex emotional landscapes. Arhaan's journey was marked by a series of experiences that shaped his understanding of relationships and personal growth.

In the end, the interaction with Alankrita was a chapter in Arhaan's story, one that contributed to his overall development and self-awareness. It was a reminder that life's challenges and uncertainties are part of a larger process of growth and understanding. As he moved forward, Arhaan remained committed to his goals and aspirations, embracing the lessons learned from his experiences and looking forward to the future with a sense of purpose and determination.

Chapter 16

New Beginnings: A Tech Entrepreneur Emerges

Years had passed in the blink of an eye, and Arhaan had undergone a remarkable transformation. The boy who once entered a new school with a mixture of hope and uncertainty had grown into a man who exuded confidence and charm. His journey through these years was marked by significant personal and professional changes, reflecting the growth and evolution that had shaped him into the person he had become.

Arhaan's physical appearance had changed considerably since his school days. The chubby, average-looking boy had shed his previous physique, emerging as a strikingly handsome young man. His dedication to improving himself was evident in his refined appearance. He had worked diligently to reduce his weight and enhance his overall fitness. The results were not only visible but also spoke to his commitment to personal development.

Gone was the slightly curly hair that once framed his

face. In its place was a more polished, well-groomed style that complemented his new look. His fair skin, once marked by youthful softness, now radiated a healthy glow that accentuated his features. His bright eyes, filled with passion and ambition, were a testament to the years of hard work and dedication he had invested in his personal and professional growth.

Arhaan's transformation went beyond mere appearance. His charm and charisma had matured, reflecting his newfound self-assuredness. He had evolved from a boy who felt average and overlooked into a confident, attractive young man who carried himself with grace and poise. This change was not just superficial; it represented the culmination of his efforts to become the best version of himself.

After graduating, Arhaan ventured into the professional world with a clear sense of purpose and ambition. He chose to pursue a career in the tech industry, driven by a passion for innovation and technology. His academic background and personal experiences had prepared him well for this new chapter of his life.

Arhaan's journey into the tech industry was marked by a series of accomplishments and milestones. He quickly established himself as a promising entrepreneur, driven by a vision to create and innovate. His work ethic, combined with his technical skills and creativity, allowed him to make significant strides in his chosen field.

He immersed himself in the world of technology, exploring new ideas, developing cutting-edge solutions, and contributing to projects that had a meaningful impact. Arhaan's dedication to his work was evident in the success he achieved and the respect he garnered from colleagues and peers. His entrepreneurial spirit was a driving force behind his accomplishments, and he continued to push boundaries and explore new horizons.

As Arhaan's professional life flourished, so did the landscape of social media. The technological advancements that had shaped his career also influenced the ways in which people connected and interacted online. The rapid evolution of social media platforms mirrored the changes in Arhaan's life, highlighting the dynamic nature of technology and communication.

One of the significant developments in the realm of social media was the rise of a new platform named Instaconnect. Unlike its predecessors, Instaconnect offered a fresh and innovative approach to connecting with others. It became highly popular among Arhaan's friends and colleagues, providing a space for sharing experiences, updates, and professional achievements.

Arhaan was intrigued by Instaconnect and decided to create his profile on the platform. He saw it as an opportunity to reconnect with old friends, share his own journey, and engage with a broader network of individuals. The platform's user-friendly interface and engaging features made it an appealing choice for staying connected in a rapidly changing digital landscape.

As Arhaan set up his profile on Instaconnect, he was filled with a sense of excitement and anticipation. The platform offered a chance to reconnect with people from his past, including friends from school and early professional contacts. The ability to share updates, photos, and personal milestones on Instaconnect allowed Arhaan to bridge the gap between his past and present.

One of the most fulfilling aspects of creating his profile was the opportunity to reach out to old friends and acquaintances. Arhaan eagerly searched for familiar names and faces, sending friend requests and reconnecting with those he had lost touch with over the years. The process of reestablishing connections was both nostalgic and gratifying, as it allowed him to reflect on the journey he had taken and the people who had been a part of it.

Arhaan's interactions on Instaconnect were characterized by a sense of joy and nostalgia. He received messages and comments from friends who were delighted to hear from him and catch up on his life. The platform facilitated meaningful conversations, allowing Arhaan to share his experiences and listen to the stories of others.

The joy of reconnecting with old friends was amplified by the visual nature of Instaconnect. Arhaan could share photos and updates that captured the essence of his journey. Whether it was a snapshot of a recent accomplishment or a candid moment from his personal life, the ability to visually communicate his experiences added a new dimension to his connections.

As Arhaan navigated the evolving world of social media and technology, he found himself reflecting on the changes that had taken place in his life. The passage of time had brought about significant transformations, both personally and professionally. The contrast between his past and present was a testament to the growth and development he had experienced.

Arhaan's journey from a chubby, average boy to a successful entrepreneur was a source of pride and fulfillment. The changes in his appearance and career were emblematic of his dedication to self-improvement and his commitment to achieving his goals. The evolution of social media mirrored his own evolution, highlighting the interconnectedness of technology and personal growth.

The process of reconnecting with old friends on Instaconnect was a reminder of the importance of maintaining relationships and cherishing the connections that had shaped his life. Arhaan's interactions on the platform were not just about staying in touch but also about celebrating the milestones and memories that had defined his journey.

As Arhaan continued to navigate his career and personal life, he remained mindful of the lessons he had learned along the way. The changes in his appearance, career, and social connections were part of a broader narrative of growth and self-discovery. The evolution of technology and social media was a reflection of the dynamic nature of life, and Arhaan embraced these changes with a sense of optimism and curiosity.

Instaconnect became more than just a social media platform for Arhaan; it was a symbol of the new opportunities and connections that lay ahead. As he engaged with his old friends and colleagues, he looked forward to the future with a sense of excitement and possibility. The journey of reconnecting and reflecting on the past was a reminder of the importance of staying connected and embracing the changes that come with time.

In the end, Arhaan's story was one of transformation and resilience. The passage of years had brought about significant changes, both in his personal appearance and professional achievements. The evolution of social media and technology had mirrored his own growth, highlighting the interconnectedness of life and the importance of embracing change.

As Arhaan continued to pursue his ambitions and navigate the evolving landscape of technology, he remained committed to his goals and aspirations. The experiences of the past and the opportunities of the future were intertwined, shaping his journey and guiding him toward new horizons.

Chapter 17

Blocked Again: The Unexpected Digital Wall

In the evolving world of social media, connections and interactions had taken on a new form. Platforms like Instaconnect had become integral to daily life, offering a digital space where people could maintain relationships, share their lives, and connect with old friends. Arhaan, having embraced the technological advancements of the time, was an active user of Instaconnect. The platform had allowed him to reconnect with numerous acquaintances from his past, including those from his school days.

Among these connections was Alankrita. Arhaan had been aware of her presence on Instaconnect, and the knowledge that she was on the same platform as him stirred a complex mix of emotions. The digital space was both a bridge and a barrier—a place where reconnections were possible yet fraught with uncertainty. Arhaan's feelings towards Alankrita, a mixture of nostalgia and unresolved emotions, created a hesitancy that prevented him from reaching out.

Arhaan's hesitation to connect with Alankrita was deeply rooted in his complex emotions. The years had not diminished his feelings for her; if anything, they had become more intense as he had reflected on their shared past and the connection they once had. Despite his progress and growth, the emotional weight of his unspoken feelings remained.

He had grappled with the decision to reach out, torn between the desire to reconnect and the fear of disrupting the delicate balance of their memories. The fear of rejection or a negative response had held him back. In the digital age, where messages and friend requests could easily be ignored or dismissed, the risk of an awkward interaction loomed large. Thus, he chose to remain in the shadows of Instaconnect, observing from afar but not daring to initiate contact.

After two years of silence, Arhaan decided to overcome his hesitancy and make an attempt to reconnect with Alankrita. The passage of time had given him a sense of clarity and resolve. He felt ready to bridge the gap that had existed between them, driven by a combination of curiosity and a lingering hope of rekindling some form of connection.

The decision to send a friend request was not made lightly. It was accompanied by a mix of anticipation and trepidation. Arhaan had hoped that reaching out might offer some closure or even the possibility of reigniting a friendship. The process of sending the request was straightforward, but the emotional weight behind it was significant.

Instaconnect, like many social media platforms, offered users the choice between public and private profiles. Arhaan's profile was set to public, meaning that his posts, photos, and updates were visible to anyone who visited his profile. This setting allowed his content to be accessible to a wide audience, including anyone who searched for him or came across his profile through mutual connections.

In contrast, Alankrita's profile was set to private. This meant that only her approved followers could view her content. The privacy setting was a deliberate choice, reflecting her preference to keep her personal life more controlled and secure. Unlike Arhaan's public profile, Alankrita's private account required a friend request to access her posts and updates. Without such access, Arhaan was unable to view her content or understand her current life circumstances.

The distinction between their profile settings highlighted the dynamics of their online interactions. While Arhaan's public profile made his life open and accessible, Alankrita's private profile created a barrier that restricted his ability to connect with her. This disparity in profile visibility added to the complexity of their digital relationship and the eventual outcome of their interaction.

To Arhaan's astonishment, his attempt to reconnect was met with an unexpected and disheartening response. When he checked Instaconnect after sending the friend request, he discovered that Alankrita had blocked him. The revelation was a jarring blow. The action of being blocked was not just a digital gesture; it was a clear statement that Alankrita had chosen to sever the possibility of any interaction.

The fact that Alankrita's account was private added another layer of complexity to the situation. While Arhaan's profile was public, allowing anyone to view his posts and updates, Alankrita's private account meant that her content was inaccessible to him. Despite this, the act of blocking was particularly striking because it indicated a deliberate and definitive choice to exclude him from her digital space.

The blocking of Arhaan's profile, coupled with the privacy of Alankrita's account, meant that he could no longer attempt to connect or follow her updates. The emotional impact of this was compounded by the knowledge that he had no means of understanding her reasons or seeking closure. The lack of access to her content and the absence of any communication further heightened the sense of rejection and confusion.

The shock of being blocked was profound for Arhaan. It was more than just a moment of confusion; it was a blow to his self-esteem and an unsettling reminder of unresolved feelings. The reasons behind the block were unclear, and the lack of explanation left Arhaan grappling with unanswered questions. He had hoped for a different outcome, one where a simple friend request might lead to a renewed connection or at least some form of communication.

The unexpected block forced Arhaan to confront the reality of their situation. It was a stark reminder that his past relationship with Alankrita was now a closed chapter, at least in the context of their digital interactions. The digital rejection felt personal, amplifying the emotions of sadness and confusion that Arhaan experienced.

In the aftermath of the block, Arhaan found himself reflecting on the events and his own feelings. The digital rejection prompted a period of introspection, during which he sought to understand the reasons behind Alankrita's decision. He considered whether there had been any signals or signs that he might have missed, but the lack of communication made it difficult to draw any conclusions.

The experience also led Arhaan to reevaluate his

approach to relationships and connections. He realized that despite his efforts to reconnect, the past was not always a place where resolutions could be found. The digital world, while offering opportunities for reconnection, could also reinforce the finality of certain relationships.

The block on Instaconnect became a defining moment for Arhaan, marking a shift in his perspective. He acknowledged that while the digital space had its limitations, it also provided a valuable lesson in accepting the boundaries of personal connections. The incident reinforced the importance of moving forward and focusing on the present and future.

Arhaan channeled his emotions into his work and personal growth. The shock of the block, while painful, became a catalyst for him to concentrate on his professional goals and aspirations. He redirected his energy towards his career and continued to build on the achievements he had made in the tech industry.

The experience of being blocked on Instaconnect was a reminder that not all connections could be revived, and some relationships were meant to remain in the past. It underscored the importance of accepting and respecting the choices of others, even when they diverge from one's own expectations or desires.

As Arhaan navigated the complexities of digital interactions and personal growth, the block on Instaconnect remained a poignant chapter in his journey. The unexpected rejection highlighted the nuanced nature of modern relationships and the challenges of reconciling past connections with the present. While the experience was disheartening, it served as a reminder of the importance of moving forward and embracing the opportunities that lay ahead.

The digital landscape had evolved, and with it, so had Arhaan's understanding of relationships and connections. The block on Instaconnect was a significant event, but it was also a part of a larger narrative of growth, acceptance, and self-discovery. As Arhaan continued to pursue his ambitions and navigate the evolving world of technology and social media, he carried with him the lessons learned from this experience, shaping his approach to future relationships and opportunities.

Chapter 18

Acceptance: Moving Ahead with Maturity

After discovering that Alankrita had blocked him on Instaconnect, Arhaan found himself grappling with a wave of emotions he hadn't anticipated. The initial shock was overwhelming, but as the days passed, it slowly gave way to a quiet resignation. The unanswered questions and lingering doubts gnawed at him, yet Arhaan knew he had to move forward, even if the path ahead seemed unclear.

The realization that Alankrita had chosen to sever any potential connection with him felt like a final blow to his lingering hopes. For years, he had nurtured a deep affection for her, a feeling that had grown from a simple infatuation into something far more profound. But now, faced with the reality of her decision, Arhaan had to confront the possibility that their relationship, whatever it might have been, was truly over.

Arhaan's heart was heavy, burdened by the weight of unspoken words and unrealized dreams. The pain of unreciprocated love is one of the most difficult burdens to bear, and for Arhaan, it was no different. Despite all his efforts to move on, the memories of Alankrita remained etched in his mind, refusing to fade away.

He often found himself revisiting the past, replaying moments they had shared, wondering if there had been any signs he had missed, any indication that things would eventually come to this. The block on Instaconnect wasn't just a digital action; it was a symbolic end to the chapter of his life that Alankrita had been a part of. It forced him to confront the reality that some things, no matter how deeply desired, were simply not meant to be.

Yet, with time, Arhaan began to understand that this was a necessary step in his journey toward self-discovery and growth. Life, he realized, doesn't always go according to plan. There are moments when one must accept that not every dream can be fulfilled, not every desire can be met. This understanding didn't come easily to him; it was the result of many sleepless nights, introspective days, and long walks alone, where he would lose himself in thought.

The maturity that came with this understanding was hard-won. Arhaan had always been someone who believed in fighting for what he wanted, in pursuing his dreams with relentless determination. But this was different. This was a lesson in acceptance, in understanding that some battles are lost not because of a lack of effort, but because they are not meant to be won.

It was during this period of reflection that Arhaan began to channel his energy into his work. The tech industry was a fast-paced and demanding field, one that required constant innovation, creativity, and dedication. For Arhaan, it became a sanctuary of sorts, a place where he could lose himself in the complexities of coding, the challenges of design, and the thrill of creating something new. The work demanded his full attention, leaving little room for the thoughts of Alankrita that once occupied his mind so frequently.

In the quiet hours of the night, when he sat alone in his

apartment, staring at the code on his computer screen, Arhaan found a sense of peace in the rhythm of his work. The endless lines of code were a puzzle to be solved, a challenge to be met, and in them, he found a way to channel his emotions productively. It was through this focus on his career that Arhaan began to rebuild his sense of self, independent of the love he had lost.

As the months turned into years, Arhaan's professional success began to grow. His hard work and dedication paid off as he steadily climbed the ranks in his field, earning recognition for his innovative ideas and leadership skills. The company he worked for thrived under his guidance, and soon, he was known as one of the most promising young entrepreneurs in the tech industry.

But despite his professional achievements, there was still a part of Arhaan that struggled with the pain of the past. He had come to terms with the fact that he might never understand why Alankrita had blocked him, why she had chosen to distance herself from him in such a final way. The lack of closure was something he had to learn to live with, a wound that would never fully heal.

In his heart, Arhaan knew that he would never forget Alankrita. She had been a significant part of his life, a source of inspiration, and someone who had shaped him in ways he couldn't fully articulate. But he also knew that holding on to the past would only hinder his progress, would only keep him trapped in a cycle of longing and regret. And so, he made a conscious decision to let go, to focus on the future and the possibilities it held.

This decision wasn't easy. There were moments when the memories would flood back, unbidden, bringing with them a rush of emotions that threatened to overwhelm him. But each time, Arhaan reminded himself of the lessons he had learned, of the maturity he had gained, and of the goals he had set for himself. He was determined to build a life that he could be proud of, a life that wasn't defined by the love he had lost but by the achievements he had yet to accomplish.

The pain of unrequited love had given way to a sense

of purpose, a drive to succeed in a world that was constantly evolving. Arhaan threw himself into his work with renewed vigor, using his experiences to fuel his ambition and creativity. He became a leader in his field, not just because of his technical skills, but because of the resilience he had developed, the ability to persevere in the face of adversity.

Arhaan's journey was far from over. There would be new challenges to face, new obstacles to overcome, but he was ready for them. He had learned that life was unpredictable, that it could take unexpected turns, but he had also learned that he was capable of navigating those turns, of finding his way even when the path was unclear.

As Arhaan continued to build his career, he found that the pain of the past began to fade, replaced by a sense of fulfillment that came from achieving his goals and pursuing his passion. He knew that the memories of Alankrita would always be a part of him, but they no longer held the same power over him that they once had. He had found a way to move forward, to create a future that was bright and full of promise.

In the end, Arhaan realized that life was about more than just love. It was about growth, about learning from experiences, and about finding a way to thrive even when things didn't go as planned. He had endured the pain of loss, but he had also discovered the strength within himself to rise above it, to build a life that was meaningful and fulfilling.

And so, with a heart that had been tempered by time and experience, Arhaan stepped into the future with confidence, ready to face whatever challenges lay ahead. He knew that there would be more to learn, more to achieve, and more to experience, but he was no longer afraid. He had found his way, and he was determined to make the most of the opportunities that life presented to him.

The chapter of his life that had been defined by Alankrita was now closed, but it had given way to a new chapter, one filled with potential and possibility. And as Arhaan looked ahead, he knew that he was ready for whatever the future had in store for him.

Chapter 19

A Peak of Success: The Unexpected Visitor

Years had passed since Arhaan had made the difficult decision to move forward with his life, despite the lingering feelings he had for Alankrita. He had come to understand that life doesn't always give you what you desire most, but that didn't mean he would let it define him. In the years following his realization, Arhaan poured all his energy, creativity, and ambition into his professional life. He worked tirelessly, driven by an intense desire to succeed, not just for himself but for the idea that had taken root in his mind during his college years.

Arhaan had always had a passion for music and technology. He saw the potential for a fusion of these two worlds, believing that technology could transform the music industry in ways that had never been done before. With this vision, he set out to create a brand that would marry the two, offering cutting-edge technology solutions for music production, distribution, and performance. His brand, which he named Sonic Pulse, was built on the principles of innovation, creativity, and accessibility. Sonic Pulse didn't just cater to established artists but provided tools and platforms for up-and-coming musicians to create and share their work with the world.

His journey was anything but easy. The music industry was fiercely competitive, and the technology sector moved at a pace that could be difficult to keep up with. But Arhaan was relentless. He surrounded himself with a team of like-minded individuals who shared his passion and drive, and together, they pushed the boundaries of what was possible. Over time, Sonic Pulse became more than just a company; it became a movement. Arhaan's leadership, creativity, and unyielding dedication to his vision turned Sonic Pulse into a brand that was respected and admired across the industry.

By the time Arhaan was in his late twenties, Sonic Pulse had grown into a massive franchise, with branches in major cities around the world. They had developed state-of-the-art music production software, designed innovative instruments, and created platforms that allowed artists to connect with their audiences in new and exciting ways. Arhaan's brand had become synonymous with the future of music, and he had become a role model for aspiring entrepreneurs and musicians alike.

As Sonic Pulse thrived, so did Arhaan. The relentless pursuit of his dreams had shaped him into a man who exuded confidence and strength. His appearance was the very embodiment of discipline and determination. He was no longer the slightly awkward, unsure young man he had been in school. Years of hard work had honed not just his mind but his body as well. Arhaan now had a well-built physique that spoke of strength and discipline. His fair skin had taken on a healthy glow, and his once-boyish features had matured into those of a handsome, confident man. His face, now more chiseled and defined, was striking, with sharp cheekbones, a strong jawline, and a pair of deep, expressive eyes that seemed to hold a world of knowledge and experience. These eyes, once filled with the innocence of youth, now gleamed with the confidence of a man who had faced challenges head-on and emerged victorious.

Arhaan's wardrobe had also evolved, reflecting his newfound status and confidence. He now favored tailored suits that complemented his well-built frame, exuding an air of authority and sophistication. He had become the kind of man who turned heads when he walked into a room, not just because of his appearance but because of the aura of success and determination that surrounded him.

One day, as Arhaan sat in his office—a sleek, modern space that reflected the innovative spirit of Sonic Pulse—he was deep in thought, going over the details of a new project they were about to launch. His office was located on the top floor of the Sonic Pulse headquarters, a building that stood as a testament to his journey from a dreamer to a visionary leader. The walls were adorned with accolades, awards, and framed photographs that captured moments from the company's rise to prominence. Behind his desk was a large window that offered a panoramic view of the city, a constant reminder of how far he had come.

As he worked, the intercom on his desk buzzed, interrupting his concentration. It was his assistant, a young woman named Riya who had been with him since the early days of Sonic Pulse.

"Mr. Arhaan, there's someone here to see you," Riya's voice came through the speaker. "She says it's important."

Arhaan glanced at the clock on his desk. It was late in the afternoon, and he didn't have any appointments scheduled. He wasn't expecting anyone. His mind quickly ran through the possibilities—perhaps it was a business partner, or maybe a journalist seeking an interview.

"Who is it?" Arhaan asked, his voice calm but curious.

"She didn't give her name," Riya replied. "But she insists that she needs to see you."

Arhaan frowned slightly. It wasn't unusual for people

to show up unannounced, but it was rare for someone to refuse to give their name. He considered for a moment, then decided to go ahead and meet the visitor. After all, whoever it was had come all the way to his office, and it might be something important.

"Alright, send her in," Arhaan said, leaning back in his chair, his curiosity piqued.

He stood up from his desk, adjusting the cuffs of his shirt as he did so. His office was spacious, with a large, dark wood desk in the center, a plush leather chair behind it, and a comfortable seating area for guests. The walls were painted in soft, neutral tones, and the decor was minimalistic yet elegant. A few moments later, the door to his office opened, and Riya stepped inside, holding the door open for the visitor.

Arhaan turned his attention to the door, expecting to see a business associate or perhaps a fan of Sonic Pulse. But the moment he saw the woman who stepped into his office, his breath caught in his throat.

It was Alankrita.

For a few seconds, Arhaan stood frozen, his mind struggling to process what he was seeing. He hadn't seen her in years, not since the time she had inexplicably blocked him on social media. He had moved on, or at least he had convinced himself that he had. He had thrown himself into his work, building Sonic Pulse from the ground up, focusing on his ambitions, and letting go of the past—or so he thought.

But now, here she was, standing in his office, looking as beautiful as ever. The years had been kind to Alankrita. She had matured into a woman of grace and elegance, her features more refined but still carrying the same charm that had once captivated him. Her long, dark hair framed her face perfectly, and her eyes— those same eyes that had once made his heart race— held a mixture of emotions that he couldn't quite decipher.

Arhaan felt a surge of emotions rush through him, emotions he had thought were long buried. The sight of Alankrita standing before him brought back memories he had pushed to the back of his mind—memories of their friendship, the times they had spent together, and the feelings he had harbored for her. He remembered the confession he had made through a message, and the silence that had followed. He remembered the disappointment, the heartbreak, and the eventual acceptance that they were never meant to be.

And yet, despite everything, seeing her again stirred something deep within him. He had become a different man over the years—stronger, more confident, and focused on his goals. But the sight of Alankrita brought a wave of vulnerability that he hadn't felt in a long time.

For a moment, they simply stared at each other, neither of them speaking. The air between them was thick with unspoken words and unresolved feelings. Arhaan could feel his heart pounding in his chest, a mixture of shock, confusion, and an old, familiar longing.

But before he could say anything, before he could even gather his thoughts, the chapter of this encounter ended. The moment stretched on, frozen in time, as

Arhaan took in the reality of Alankrita's presence. There were no words exchanged, no explanations given. Just the two of them, standing in the office that had become a symbol of his success, facing each other after all these years.

Arhaan had no idea what she was doing here, what she wanted to say, or why she had chosen this moment to reappear in his life. All he knew was that the past he had tried so hard to move on from had suddenly come rushing back, and he was once again standing at the crossroads of emotions he thought he had left behind.

Chapter 20

A Walk Down Memory Lane: The Park Encounter

As the door to his office closed behind him, Arhaan leaned against the wall, taking a deep breath. The brief but intense encounter with Alankrita had left him in a daze. His thoughts raced, memories flooding back as if triggered by her sudden reappearance. The entire afternoon had been a whirlwind, and the encounter was far from what he had expected. He knew he had to process the overwhelming emotions and face the reality of the moment.

He had watched her from his office window as she stood in the lobby, waiting for him, her posture calm and composed. It had been years since they had last seen each other, and the transformation was striking. Alankrita had evolved into a stunning woman, her appearance reflecting the grace and poise she had always possessed.

Alankrita now stood before him, a vision of elegance. Her long, silky black hair cascaded down her back, catching the light and giving her an almost ethereal glow. Her fair complexion had a soft, natural radiance, accentuated by a hint of pink on her cheeks. Her eyes, still as captivating as he remembered, were framed by long, dark lashes and sparkled with a depth of emotion and wisdom. Her face, once youthful and delicate, had matured into a charming, serene beauty, and her pleasant voice had a melodic quality that resonated with warmth and familiarity.

Arhaan struggled to reconcile this poised, sophisticated woman with the girl he had known from school. He tried to keep his composure, though his heart was pounding. The brief moment of stunned silence was interrupted by a soft, almost hesitant smile from Alankrita.

"Hi, Arhaan," she said, her voice gentle, with a hint of nostalgia.

He managed a smile in return, though his mind was still trying to catch up with the reality of her presence. "Hi, Alankrita. I... didn't expect to see you here."

"I know," she said softly, her eyes meeting his with an earnest expression. "I was surprised too. But I'm glad we finally met again."

Their initial exchange was polite, almost formal, as if they were both trying to navigate the sea of emotions that had resurfaced. Arhaan gestured towards the door. "How about we take a walk? There's a park nearby. It might be nice to catch up."

Alankrita nodded, her smile widening. "I'd like that."

They stepped out of the office building and into the crisp, late afternoon air. The park was just a short walk away, nestled among the city's high-rises like a tranquil oasis. The path was lined with trees whose leaves rustled softly in the breeze, and the sun was beginning its descent, casting a warm, golden hue over the landscape.

As they walked, the tension between them slowly began to dissolve, replaced by the ease of old friends reconnecting. The familiar surroundings of the park seemed to help bridge the years that had passed.

Arhaan glanced at Alankrita, noting how her presence seemed to bring an unexpected sense of comfort and familiarity.

"So, how have you been?" Arhaan asked, his voice tinged with genuine curiosity.

"I've been well," Alankrita replied, her tone relaxed. "I'm an artist now, teaching arts and drawing. It's been fulfilling, though challenging at times. What about you?"

"Congratulations on your career," Arhaan said, genuinely impressed. "I've been working in the tech industry. My company, Sonic Pulse, has been growing, and we've been working on some exciting projects. It's been a lot of hard work, but rewarding."

They continued to walk, discussing their respective journeys and the paths they had taken since their last meeting. The conversation flowed easily, as though no time had passed at all. They reminisced about their school days, laughing about the silly things they used to do and sharing stories about their lives since then.

"Do you remember that time we had to work on that group project together?" Alankrita said with a laugh. "I was so nervous about it."

Arhaan chuckled. "Yes, I remember. You were worried about everything, but you ended up being the star of the project. Your presentation was brilliant."

Alankrita's eyes sparkled with amusement. "And you were always the calm one, handling everything with ease."

Their laughter was a pleasant reminder of the bond they had once shared, and Arhaan couldn't help but feel a pang of longing for those simpler times. As they strolled through the park, the sun continued its descent, casting longer shadows and painting the sky with hues of orange and pink.

Their conversation turned more reflective as they began to discuss more personal matters. "Have you ever thought about where life takes us after all these years?" Alankrita asked thoughtfully. "Sometimes I wonder how different things might have been if we'd stayed in touch more."

Arhaan nodded. "I've thought about that too. Life has a way of leading us down unexpected paths. But meeting you again now, it's like seeing a piece of my past come alive."

Alankrita smiled warmly, her gaze fixed on the horizon. "It's strange, isn't it? How certain people can leave such a lasting impact on our lives?"

"Yes, it is," Arhaan agreed. "You've always been one of those people for me. Even after all these years, I find myself thinking about the moments we shared."

The park was growing quieter as the day gave way to evening. The sun was setting, and the sky was painted with deepening shades of twilight. They found a bench near a small pond, where the gentle ripples reflected the colors of the sky. The serene atmosphere seemed to enhance their sense of connection.

As they sat together on the bench, the conversation began to wind down. The air grew cooler, and the first stars began to appear in the sky. It was in this tranquil setting that Arhaan felt a subtle shift in the atmosphere between them. The ease and comfort they had established now seemed to give way to a deeper, more poignant emotional connection.

Alankrita looked at Arhaan, her expression soft and contemplative. "You know, I've been thinking a lot about what's important in life. Sometimes we get so caught up in our ambitions and goals that we forget to appreciate the people who matter to us."

Arhaan met her gaze, feeling a surge of emotion. "I understand what you mean. I've been so focused on my career that I didn't realize how much I missed having you in my life."

The silence that followed was filled with unspoken feelings. Arhaan could feel the weight of their shared history and the unaddressed emotions that had been lingering between them. It was a moment of vulnerability, a time when both of them were fully aware of the significance of their reunion.

Without warning, Alankrita reached out and took

Arhaan's hand in hers. The gesture was gentle, yet it conveyed a depth of emotion that words could not fully capture. Her touch was warm and comforting, and for a moment, time seemed to stand still.

Arhaan looked down at their joined hands, his heart racing. He felt a mixture of astonishment and profound connection. The simple act of holding hands was laden with meaning, a silent acknowledgment of the feelings that had always existed between them.

As the twilight deepened and the park grew darker, their hands remained entwined, a symbol of the bond that had never truly faded. The evening was drawing to a close, and the stars above began to twinkle more brightly, mirroring the emotions that had resurfaced between them.

In that serene, twilight moment, with Alankrita's hand in his, Arhaan felt a sense of completeness that he hadn't experienced in years. It was as if the universe had conspired to bring them back together, to remind them of the connection they had shared and the feelings that had never completely vanished.

As the sun dipped below the horizon and the park was bathed in the soft glow of the evening, Arhaan and Alankrita sat together in silence, savouring the simple, yet profound, moment of being together once more.

Chapter 21

The Revelation: Love and Sorrow Unveiled

As the twilight deepened and the park settled into the gentle embrace of night, Arhaan and Alankrita sat together on the bench, their hands still intertwined. The sky, now a deep indigo, was punctuated by the first glimmers of starlight. The park, once a bustling refuge of natural beauty, was now quiet, save for the occasional rustle of leaves in the evening breeze.

The silence between them was filled with unspoken words and emotions that had been building for years. Arhaan's heart was pounding in his chest, a tumultuous mix of anticipation and trepidation. The simple, yet profound, act of holding hands seemed to have unlocked a floodgate of memories and feelings, and he was bracing himself for what was to come.

Alankrita turned to face Arhaan, her expression a mixture of sadness and determination. Her eyes, which had sparkled with warmth earlier, now reflected a depth of sorrow and vulnerability. It was as though she had gathered all her courage to reveal something that had been weighing heavily on her heart.

"Arhaan," she began softly, her voice trembling slightly, "there's something I need to tell you. I've loved you since the day we first met."

Her confession, though unexpected, was not entirely shocking. Arhaan had always sensed a deeper connection between them, even if he had never fully understood or acknowledged it. But the weight of her words was heavy, and he could feel the gravity of the moment.

"I've loved you for a long time," Alankrita continued, her gaze fixed on their joined hands. "But we can't be together. I didn't want to hurt you, so I kept my distance."

Arhaan's heart sank at her words. "Why did you block me then? Why did you push me away if you had these feelings?"

The question hung in the air, charged with a mixture of hurt and confusion. Alankrita took a deep breath, her eyes closing briefly as she struggled to find the right words. When she spoke again, her voice was soft but steady, each word laced with a profound sense of vulnerability.

"I didn't want to hurt you," she said quietly, her eyes meeting his with a painful honesty. "I have a fatal disease, something I've been living with since I was fourteen years old. I've been on medication for years, but the doctors told me that if it's not cured, I might not survive into my thirties."

The revelation hit Arhaan like a physical blow. His mind struggled to process the information, the weight of Alankrita's words crashing down on him. The world seemed to blur around him, and he felt as though he was sinking into a nightmarish reality.

Alankrita's voice continued, though it felt distant and muffled to Arhaan. "I didn't want to burden you with this. I wanted to protect you from the pain and uncertainty of my condition. That's why I blocked you and kept my distance. I thought it would be better for both of us if I stayed away."

Arhaan was stunned into silence. The revelation about Alankrita's illness was devastating, and he could barely comprehend the depth of her suffering. He could see the pain etched into her face, the anguish that had been part of her life for so long. It was as if the emotional and physical toll of her condition had been woven into the very fabric of her being.

Alankrita's journey had been one of resilience and courage. Despite the shadow of her illness hanging over her, she had pursued her passion for art with unwavering dedication. She had become an artist by profession, finding solace and fulfillment in teaching arts and drawing. Her love for art was not just a career choice but a vital part of her identity, a way to express herself and find meaning in her life.

She had channeled her pain and experiences into her work, using art as a medium to cope with the emotional and physical struggles she faced. Teaching art allowed her to connect with others, to share her passion and inspire her students. It was a way for her to find purpose and joy despite the challenges she endured.

As Arhaan listened to Alankrita's story, he could see the strength and determination that had driven her to pursue her dreams despite her illness. Her ability to continue living with such grace and dedication was both admirable and heartbreaking.

The evening air was cool, and the sky above was now a deep, dark blue, with the stars twinkling softly. The park seemed to hold its breath, as if it too was waiting for Arhaan's response. The silence between them was filled with the weight of the revelation and the unspoken emotions that followed.

Arhaan's mind was a whirlwind of thoughts and feelings. He had loved Alankrita for so long, and the realization of her suffering added a new layer of complexity to his emotions. The image of the vibrant, determined woman he had known was now intertwined with the image of someone who had been living with a constant, unspoken struggle.

He could barely process the gravity of what she had told him. The shock was overwhelming, and his heart ached with a mix of empathy, sorrow, and confusion.

The thought of losing her, of her suffering in silence, was almost too much to bear.

"I… I don't know what to say," Arhaan finally managed, his voice trembling. "This is all so overwhelming. I had no idea you were going through this."

Alankrita's eyes were filled with tears, and she nodded, her expression one of resignation and acceptance. "I know. It's not something I could easily share. I wanted to protect you from the pain, from the uncertainty of my condition. I didn't want to hold you back or make you suffer along with me."

Arhaan felt a surge of emotions—anger at the injustice of her situation, sorrow for her suffering, and a deep, aching love for the person before him. He wanted to comfort her, to be there for her in whatever way he could. The thought of losing her was unbearable, and the pain of seeing her struggle was almost too much to comprehend.

The evening grew darker, and the park was now bathed

in the soft glow of streetlights. The shadows seemed to mirror the emotional darkness that had settled over them. Alankrita's confession had changed everything, and the future seemed uncertain and daunting.

As Arhaan sat beside her, holding her hand, he felt a profound sense of helplessness. He wanted to offer solace and support, but the weight of her illness was something beyond his control. He could see the courage and strength in her, but it was tempered by the harsh reality of her condition.

Chapter 22

The Final Farewell: Love's Lasting Legacy

The night had settled softly over the city, the kind of night where the world feels still, as if holding its breath. Arhaan and Alankrita sat together in the dim light of the evening, their emotions raw and unfiltered. The park, where they had once shared so many memories, now served as the backdrop for a final chapter in their story, a chapter that was filled with profound sadness and poignant beauty.

The days following Alankrita's revelation were a whirlwind of emotions for Arhaan. His heart, which had once been full of hope and ambition, was now burdened with the weight of his love for Alankrita and the harsh reality of her illness. He had thrown himself into trying to help her, using all the resources and connections at his disposal, determined to find a cure, to do anything that might give her more time.

The truth, however, was a cruel reminder of life's limitations. No matter how much effort or money was invested, there were some things beyond human control. The very essence of mortality was a force that could not be tamed or purchased. Despite his best efforts, Arhaan found himself facing a bitter reality: there was no escaping the inevitability of Alankrita's fate.

Their time together during that month was a precious gift, a period of bittersweet joy amidst the looming shadow of her illness. They made the most of every moment, cherishing each day as if it were their last. Their connection deepened in ways that transcended mere words, and they built a reservoir of shared experiences and memories that would remain etched in their hearts forever.

The days were filled with moments of joy and tenderness—quiet walks in the park, late-night conversations under the stars, and simple gestures of affection that spoke volumes. Each day, they celebrated the beauty of their time together, finding solace and strength in each other's presence.

Yet, as the days passed, the inevitable approach of the

end became more palpable. The signs of Alankrita's illness grew more pronounced, and Arhaan's hope began to wane. The sight of her fragile form, once so full of life and energy, now reflected the toll of her condition. It was a painful reminder of the ephemeral nature of their time together.

On that final morning, the world outside continued its unrelenting march forward, oblivious to the personal tragedy unfolding within the confines of Arhaan and Alankrita's world. The dawn broke with a gentle light, casting a soft glow over the room where they had shared their final days. The morning air was crisp, filled with the promise of a new day, but for Arhaan, it was the beginning of an irreversible shift.

Arhaan awoke to an unsettling silence. The absence of the usual sounds that marked Alankrita's waking moments was immediately alarming. With a growing sense of dread, he turned to her, only to find that she had not stirred. His heart raced as he reached out to her, a frantic urgency driving him to confirm his worst fears.

When he realized that Alankrita had passed away, a profound sorrow overwhelmed him. The finality of her absence was a devastating blow, a stark reminder of the fragility of life and the relentless cruelty of fate. He held her close, his tears mingling with his whispers of love and regret. The grief was suffocating, a weight that seemed to crush him beneath its enormity.

In those moments, Arhaan felt as though the world had come to an abrupt halt. The love they had shared, the dreams they had nurtured, and the moments they had cherished were now a part of his past, preserved in the confines of his memory. The realization that he could no longer hold her, no longer share his life with her, was an unbearable burden.

The days following Alankrita's passing were a blur of mourning and reflection. Arhaan grappled with the profound sense of loss, struggling to come to terms with the reality of her absence. The world around him continued to spin, but for him, time seemed to stand still. The memories of their time together became both a source of comfort and a reminder of what had been lost.

He found solace in the quiet moments, reflecting on the beauty of their shared experiences and the depth of their connection. The park where they had spent so many hours now held a special significance, a place where he could go to remember her and feel her presence. The echoes of their laughter and the warmth of their conversations lingered in the air, a testament to the love that had once filled their lives.

Arhaan's journey through grief was a path marked by both pain and healing. He learned to navigate the complexities of his emotions, finding ways to honor Alankrita's memory while continuing to move forward with his life. The love they had shared became a guiding force, shaping his perspective and influencing his choices.

As he looked back on their time together, Arhaan realized that their love, though brief, had been profoundly meaningful. It had taught him the value of cherishing every moment and the importance of embracing life's uncertainties with grace and resilience.

Alankrita's spirit lived on in his heart, a source of inspiration and strength.

In the end, the story of Arhaan and Alankrita was one of enduring love and the harsh realities of life. Their time together had been a gift, a reminder of the beauty that could be found even in the face of adversity. The love they had shared, though cut short by fate, had left an indelible mark on their lives.

As the years went by, Arhaan continued to honor Alankrita's memory by living a life filled with purpose and passion. He carried her spirit with him, using the lessons he had learned from their time together to guide him in his personal and professional endeavors. The love they had shared remained a cherished part of his life, a reminder of the profound connection they had forged.

In the quiet moments of reflection, Arhaan would often return to the park where they had shared their final days. It was a place of solace and remembrance, a sanctuary where he could feel close to her and reflect on the beauty of their time together. The park, with its serene beauty and the echoes of their laughter, became a symbol of their enduring love.

The final chapter of their story was one of poignant beauty and profound sorrow. It was a testament to the strength of their love and the impact it had on their lives. Even though Alankrita was no longer physically present, her memory lived on in the heart of the man who had loved her deeply and cherished every moment they had shared.

As Arhaan looked out over the park, he felt a sense of peace and acceptance. The pain of her loss was still there, but it was tempered by the knowledge that their love had been true and meaningful. The memories of their time together, the moments of joy and sorrow, had shaped him into the person he had become.

In the end, Arhaan found solace in the realization that love, even in its most fleeting form, could leave a lasting impact. The story of Arhaan and Alankrita was a reminder that life, with all its trials and tribulations, was also filled with moments of profound beauty and connection. Their love, though brief, had been a testament to the power of the human spirit and the enduring nature of the heart.

www.ingramcontent.com/pod-product-compliance
Lightning Source LLC
Chambersburg PA
CBHW031624170726
47990CB00017B/365